MURDER NEVER KNOCKS

A MIKE HAMMER NOVEL

MURDER NEVER KNOCKS

A MIKE HAMMER NOVEL

MICKEY SPILLANE
and
MAX ALLAN COLLINS

TITANBOOKS

Murder Never Knocks: A Mike Hammer Novel
Print edition ISBN: 9781783291342
E-book edition ISBN: 9781783291373

Published by Titan Books
A division of Titan Publishing Group Ltd
144 Southwark St, London SE1 0UP

First edition: March 2016

1 3 5 7 9 10 8 6 4 2

A CIP catalogue record for this title is available from the British Library.

Printed and bound in the United States.

Did you enjoy this book? We love to hear from our readers.
Please email us at readerfeedback@titanemail.com or write to us at
Reader Feedback at the above address.

To receive advance information, news, competitions, and exclusive
Titan offers online, please sign up for the Titan newsletter on our website:
www.titanbooks.com

For my writer pal

STEVE MERTZ

whose love for Mickey's work
rivals my own.

CO-AUTHOR'S NOTE

Shortly before his death, Mike Hammer's creator Mickey Spillane paid me an incredible honor. He asked me to complete the Hammer novel that he currently had in progress—*The Goliath Bone*—and then told his wife Jane to gather all of the other unfinished, unpublished material and give it to me: "Max will know what to do."

These manuscripts, surprising in number, spanned Mickey's entire career from the late '40s until his passing in 2006. Six manuscripts were substantial, usually 100 pages or more, with plot and character notes and sometimes roughed-out final chapters. Most of the books had been announced by Mickey's publisher at various times from the 1950s through the '90s. As a Spillane/Hammer fan since my early teens, I am delighted to finally see these long-promised books lined up on a shelf next to the thirteen Hammer novels published by Mickey in his lifetime.

In addition to the substantial novel manuscripts mentioned above, a number of shorter Mike Hammer manuscripts were uncovered in the treasure hunt conducted by Jane Spillane, my wife Barb and me, ranging over three offices in Mickey's South Carolina home. Some of these were fragments of a few pages, primarily the openings of never-written novels or stories; these I have been gradually turning into short stories with an eventual collection in mind. Others were more substantial if less so than the six novel manuscripts, and—although they vary in particulars—these shorter manuscripts represent significant unfinished entries in the most popular American mystery series of the twentieth century.

I am now in the process of completing at least three of these shorter Hammer novels-in-progress; *Murder Never Knocks* is the second of these (the first, *Kill Me, Darling,* appeared in 2015). Mickey had completed several chapters but also left behind extensive plot and character notes, as well as a draft of the novel's ending. Mike Hammer's creator often said that he wrote the ending first. Of the unfinished manuscripts in Mickey's files, *Murder Never Knocks* is one of the few that back up that assertion.

The alternate title, *Don't Look Behind You,* is partly a tribute by Mickey to his favorite mystery writer, Fredric Brown, who wrote a famous short story of that name. Mickey's other alternate titles were *The Controlled Kill* and *The Controller.*

Internal evidence in the narrative indicates Mickey began this novel in 1966 or 1967, before or after *The Body Lovers* (1967), and that is the time frame I've employed.

M.A.C.

CHAPTER ONE

He just stood there looking at me, the silenced, foreign-made automatic pointed at my chest, the key he had used in the door still in the fingers of his left hand until he gently dropped it in his pocket. I hadn't heard him at all. He was already framed in the doorway when I noticed him. But then, he was the kind you didn't notice.

Eight stories down, on the streets of New York, there were thousands like him, quiet people, utterly uncommanding souls who could pass unnoticed anywhere. They could be next to you on the sidewalk, or maybe behind you, without being seen, and speaking without being heard. Their faces and their actions would never be remembered except vaguely at best. Just part of the crowd.

That made him anonymous. It also pegged him a pro. Because such unremarkable people make the best killers.

This one might have been a lower level drone from Wall Street—nice gray topcoat but off the rack, a darker gray trilby hat, gray complexion, too. The only thing that stood out were the black-rimmed glasses on his narrow soft-jawed face, and the eyes behind them were gray, too.

His voice was a soft monotone, but there was something off in it. "Mike Hammer. In person. In the flesh. Hard to believe."

What was that something in his voice? Sarcasm? No. Respect? Or… awe? It was like he'd spotted his favorite movie star across a room, or was taking in the Grand Canyon or maybe Mount Rushmore.

He did have a tinge of surprise tightening his eyes. That was probably because he hadn't expected to find me in the outer office, right there in front of him, big as life, ready for death. Velda, who wasn't just my secretary but the other licensed P.I. at Michael Hammer Investigations, had left just before five for an urgent appointment.

I'd hung around to take a phone call from the West Coast, and was on my way out when I noticed a stack of afternoon mail on her desk. I perched on the edge of it, lit up a Lucky, and started thumbing through the envelopes. He'd come in and found me like that.

Casual as hell, I tossed the mail on the blotter and half-turned on my roost, took a drag from the butt and put it down in the ashtray. I gave him an easy grin, nothing nasty in it at all.

"Why hard to believe?" I asked. "I'm not tough to find."

A tiny smile. Damn, the teeth were gray, too.

"You're a tough man to find *alone*, Mr. Hammer. And when you are, you're on the move." The gun was steady as he shook his head, his smile slight but regretful. "Pity it has to be like this."

"To what do I owe this honor?"

"I have no idea why."

"You have an idea who, then? Anybody I know?"

He shook his head, his eyes never leaving mine. The automatic snout with its silencer, either. "Nobody *I* even know."

"So it's a contract job."

He nodded once. "A very lucrative one, Mr. Hammer. Not just anyone was deemed up to it. But I have to admit, I almost regret having to fulfill it."

"And why is that?"

His eyebrows went up a touch. "You may find this hard to believe, but some people on my side of this business… well, a good number of us look up to you. How many kills have you racked up by now, Mr. Hammer?"

"Who's counting?"

The unremarkable face gave up a whole gray smile now. "And to think I won't even get any credit for it." His shrug was barely perceptible. "Nature of the business. Back in the day, take out the likes of Mike Hammer, you'd be a big man. Imagine taking out Billy the Kid or Jesse James, and no one ever knew? But the world operates differently now, doesn't it?"

I picked up the butt, took another deep drag, and put it back in the tray again. "You're being pretty careless about this thing, aren't you? Shouldn't I be dead by now?"

The smile lingered. "You're not going anywhere. Would you like to know how I managed this?"

"Sure."

"I rented an office down the hall a month ago. That gave me freedom of the building. I wanted to observe your, ah… routine. Your habits. Your patterns." He saw my eyes touch his pocket. "The key is a copy of the superintendent's master. Tonight was the first time your secretary didn't double-lock your door when she left, you know."

I shrugged. "Guess she was in a hurry. Everybody screws up now and then."

This time there was a touch of pathos in the smile. "With all due respect, Mr. Hammer, some of us don't."

My hand drifted toward the cigarette in the ashtray, but the cig went flying in a shower of sparks when I flung the glass object at him with a sharpness that sent it sailing edge first right into his forehead, stunning him just as his finger was tightening on the trigger. In that same second, my right hand was drawing the .45 from its shoulder holster and firing back at him as I hit the deck, his bullet kissing a pock in the plaster behind and above me. His shot and mine were so close together, they might been one report.

But there'd be no more gunfire from my caller.

I got to my feet and had a look at him. The .45 slug had gone in clean mid-chest but delivered a fat sloppy wad of the gray man's colorful insides to splash and glop and slide bloodily down the wall behind where he lay crumpled under it, just inside the door. He looked up at me, eyes trying to blink death away. But that wasn't going to happen—not with his chest a tired beach ball, slowly deflating.

The glaze hadn't reached his eyes yet, so I'm pretty sure he could still hear me.

"I told you, buddy," I said. "Sooner or later, everybody screws up."

I had to take the hinges off the doors so they could go through the routine of seeing the body before anyone touched it. Lots of pics, lots of prints. They impounded my gun, inspected my license and took my statement while they photographed the corpse, then ushered me out when they took the guy away in a rubber body bag, neither one of us the captain of our own ship in this instance.

When we reached headquarters, the desk sergeant nodded to the detectives flanking me and said, "Chambers doesn't want to see him just yet. But keep him handy."

They dumped me on a bench outside the door that read *Captain Patrick Chambers, Homicide Division*, and somebody offered me coffee that I turned down. Instead I made the bench my hard little bed, dropped my hat down over my face and had a snooze. Killing that guy hadn't taken it out of me, but waiting around while the cops and techs treated my office like a crime scene had been a damn drain.

Somebody shook me awake, lifting the hat off my face, and it was Pat in his shirtsleeves, his tie loose as a noose awaiting a customer. I saw a tiredness that made me think maybe the hard line cop had finally mellowed out of him. Then the gray-blue eyes focused on me and I knew it hadn't.

"Up and at 'em, boy."

I yawned, sat up, tasted the nasty thickness in my mouth, and said, "What's been shaking, Pat?"

He just sighed, went over and opened his office door and I went in. The space was modest, a few filing cabinets and scads of framed citations. I took the visitor's chair while he shambled behind the desk. A couple of cardboard cups of coffee were waiting and I sampled mine.

The homicide captain laced his fingers behind his head and

leaned back in his swivel chair. His grin was as rumpled as his shirt. "Your damn luck is something else, Mike."

I shrugged.

"Your tail really ought to be hanging out on this one. Your reputation precedes you, you know. And this new administration isn't like the old one, chum. They won't be happy with you ruining the Fun City image."

"Who gives a shit?"

Pat let a small grin crease his mouth. "This time you may just get away with that flip-ass attitude. Come the inquest, you'll no doubt have a list of formidable witnesses ready to testify to your character, thanks to you getting them out of various jams."

"That's right. Haven't you heard? I'm beloved."

"Not by the new crowd you aren't. The big boys would be ready to stand you on your ear for erasing one Milton Woodcock…"

"Is that who he was?"

"…a reputable businessman from the suburbs of Chicago who recently elected to re-establish himself in the insurance game in our fair town."

"Sure," I said, "he was a nice, reputable guy all right. He came around to tell me how much he admired me while he pointed that fancy silenced rod at my chest." I shoved my hat back and slouched in the chair. "So are these big boys of yours going to lean on me or not?"

"Not." Pat took his hands down and folded them on the desk. He grunted a deep laugh and shook his head. "A dinosaur like you, and modern science gets you off the hook. That and a certain pal of yours in the Homicide Division."

"Sounds like somebody did me a favor."

"He did. I did. I rushed that foreign-make automatic through ballistics. Those boys don't like to work fast but I lit a fire."

"Thanks, buddy. When should we hear from 'em?"

"We have heard." His face drained of anything frivolous. "Woodcock had used that weapon before. He had routinely switched out the barrel so ballistics couldn't match up any slugs, but the last time out, he didn't recover all the ejected shells... and the firing pin marks tallied with the gun he held on you. I called a friend of mine on the Chicago PD, at home, and he put me in touch with a night-shift homicide dick who had a file on Mr. Woodcock as thick as your skull."

"No kidding."

"The Chicago lads were never able to indict the respectable Mr. Woodcock, but they linked him to half a dozen homicides and figured those were the tip of a very bloody iceberg. That and a few more goodies pointed to him as a contract killer, which explains his relocating to our little island."

"I should nap outside your office more often," I commented drily. "It does a taxpayer's heart good to know public servants are working like elves for him while he slumbers."

Pat spoke two words, one of them nasty, but his grin took off all the edge.

I said, "So—where do we go from here?"

The grin on Pat's mouth spread a little. "I had calls about this from two of the upstairs crowd, making lots of noise, but now they're mostly embarrassed. Woodcock's presence in our fair city is more of a liability than yours, apparently."

"So I helped keep the city clean, even if I did litter up my office. You're welcome, kiddo."

"Oh, don't get this wrong—the big shots aren't offering any apologies… but you'll walk through the inquest. In fact, I've already been instructed to return your license, gun and good name."

"Generous souls."

"Consider it a show of good faith." What he said next he tossed out casually, like a kid buying a pack of rubbers between a comb and a candy bar. "And they've given me a special assignment— investigate why you were the target of a certain contract killer."

"When you find out," I said, "be sure to let me know."

I saw the grin fade and Pat's eyes got that curious, almost spooky look I had seen so often. "Something must be running around in your mind. Like Daffy damn Duck."

I shook my head. "No way, old buddy. I haven't been on anything worth shooting me over in a long damn while. I'm just a working P.I. with a colorful reputation."

Pat waited a second, then said, "Maybe it's for something you *didn't* do."

"What is that supposed to mean?"

He shrugged. "Could be some case you got recently that you haven't dug into yet. Or maybe some client feels you didn't deliver, or maybe you did deliver and it caused somebody else trouble. This doesn't necessarily have to come from your gaudy past."

But I was waving that off. "Sorry. All my assignments for the year so far have been completed to the clients' satisfaction and none of it was anything that wasn't a simple civil case. And there's nothing shaking at all right now."

"For a guy who had a hitman caller," Pat said, "you don't seem very worried."

"Why should I be? I've been shot at before."

"You haven't been dead before. Anyway, not so you'd notice." His eyes were steady on mine. "A contract for a guy like you would come high. You've been keeping a low profile in recent years, granted, but you still have a hell of a rep."

"Thanks, buddy."

He ignored that. "The more prominent the target, the bigger the fee... but when there's a big element of possible failure involved, because the target is capable of deadly defense? Well, the price goes sky high."

My smile turned into a laugh. "When you're an aging legend, it's nice to know you're still wanted. Somebody just watched a bundle go down the drain along with the esteemed Mr. Woodcock. A contract like that would be paid in front of the kill."

"Or at least half down," Pat said, nodding. "But that much loot would mean there's plenty more where it came from. Meaning the client can afford to lay out a new bundle for another contract. So I *will* be investigating this incident, Mike. Personally. Count on it."

I wiped my hands across my eyes. It had been a long night. That snooze had been at the price of a wooden-bench backache. "And I'll do the same thing, old friend."

"That I don't like hearing. That's not your role here. You're the potential victim." His sigh started at his toes. "Could you just for once let me do my damn job, Mike?"

"Who's stopping you?"

"Well, having you to trip over around every corner is not my idea of a good time."

"It isn't much fun for me either," I told him, sitting forward, my hands clasped and draped between my legs.

His eyes narrowed. "Don't tell me it's getting to you. That this made one kill too many."

My laugh was as grating as a cough. "Are you kidding? Wiping out a punk like Woodcock doesn't strain my conscience any, Pat... but it sure can mess up an office. Cleaning blood and guts off the wall—you know the stain it'll leave? So there's a new paint job, and who pays for that? And a bullet hole in plaster, that's gonna need some work."

"Cut the comedy," Pat said.

I straightened up in the chair, tugged my hat down, and reached across the desk for my P.I. ticket and the .45 automatic that Pat shoved at me. The gun was going to need a good cleaning to get the fingerprint powder off it and one edge of my license was torn.

I said, "I guess you know the score here. The pattern."

"Let's hear your version," Pat said.

"Contract killers come in from the outside," I said. "The farther away the arrangements are made, the better. But L.A. and Frisco have their own internal problems right now, and anyway their business dealings are too closely allied with New York's to call somebody in from those locales. If your boys picked up a hitman from either city, you'd just assume the local mob was bringing in out-of-town talent, which negates the effort."

"With you so far, Mike."

"And then there's Chicago, Woodcock's former recent domicile.

That's a kind of middle ground—the windy town isn't in the pocket of the New York crime families, and plenty of talent's available there, plus the transportation options are so many you can get lost in them."

He was staring at me. "Which adds up to…?"

"The contract originating in New York."

"That's what I think," Pat said, nodding his admission.

I grinned at him. "Which means somebody around here doesn't like me." I shoved the .45 into the shoulder holster and slipped the P.I. ticket back in its plastic slot in my wallet. "And here I thought I was a beloved local institution."

"Whoever hired this thing is going to love you even less now, Mike. Taking Woodcock out means the price will go up."

"How about that?" I said.

His eyebrows climbed. "The man in the big chair at Gracie Mansion has surely been advised by now that you're potential trouble for the Big Apple."

"Am I?"

"Sure—a famous, dangerous target walking around the streets of Manhattan, just waiting to turn it into a Wild West show. Add to that, publicity about you reaches out all over the country. Right now our governor's pretty damn sensitive about his position, and his state's image."

"Screw him. I didn't vote his ticket."

"You don't vote at all, Mike." He shook his head, smiling, but there was no amusement in it. "They'll be watching for developments. The gov's got his own personal bird dogs, you know."

"Screw them too. I'm a tax-paying citizen."

"So you seem to remind me every time we get together." Pat's face turned a little grim. "Whether you're a local institution or not—or just deserve to be put in one—you are not exactly a desirable character. Our elected leaders will be waiting for just one wrong move if you go barreling out on your own."

"Is this where I bust out crying?"

Pat's face got very hard and yet something soft lingered in his eyes. "Stay out of my way on this one, okay, Mike? Just for this once?"

I got up and leaned two hands on his desk. "Buddy, if there's a contract out on me, *me* is who they'll come looking for. Not you."

"Granted, but—"

"I told you. Jump in. The water's fine—maybe a little cold this time of year. Anyway, it promises to be interesting. Do I have to tell you how I feel about this kind of thing?"

"No. I know how you think." Pat looked at me a long moment, then added, "And I know something else."

"Yeah?"

"That you can be just as bad as the bad guys yourself sometimes."

"Sometimes somebody has to," I said softly. "Sometimes you have to be worse."

He was shaking his head again. "You and that damn .45 of yours."

"It *has* been a big help, from time to time."

I started for the door. Pat's voice stopped me when my hand was on the knob. "Mike…"

"Yeah?"

"High-priced killers don't usually make mistakes."

"So I hear."

"Well, our friend Woodcock—what was his mistake?"

I grinned at him and opened the door. "He was a secret admirer of mine."

Pat goggled at me. "An *admirer?*"

"Yeah… on a professional basis. A real fan."

"So then what was his damn mistake, Mike?"

I shrugged. "He talked too much."

And I left him there to chew on that.

CHAPTER TWO

Hell, when was *the war?*

How many years ago?

You lay in the mud waiting to shoot and get shot at, and you wind up shooting a lot of people you never saw or knew and when you did a really good job of killing, you got a medal or two that you could stick in your desk drawer and look at, whenever the scarred tissue in your body told you it was going to rain. They didn't always get the little shrapnel pieces out in those field hospitals and you never really had time to deal with it after you got home. So when it rained, you remembered, and if you were me, you wondered why it was they didn't give you medals any more for killing guys who needed it.

The closest thing, over the years, had been the headlines, but that was a mixed bag. Good for business in its way, but turning you into some kind of cockeyed celebrity. To this paper you were a hero, to that one a villain or maybe even "a psychopathic menace to society." That one popped into my mind a lot, sometimes making me grin and sometimes not.

Of course, the power that was the press had been chopped down by the demands of supposedly honestly elected crooks who seemed curiously inspired to curtail the news and events from the biggest city of them all and divert them into preselected channels that didn't need direction to be cautiously liberal to the point of fear, or consciously radical enough to be dangerous.

The World Telegram *was dead, the* Journal-American *gone and the* Herald Tribune *buried, and with them the reporters and columnists, like my pal Hy Gardner, who could have laid on a rebuttal to the two papers that chewed me up without having all the facts. Somebody at the* News *had gotten the word, though, and the story was minimized and presented as an attempted murder and my action as justifiable homicide. Nobody played it up really big. Luckily, the Mid-Eastern thing was still a hot issue in the UN, so there wasn't enough space to bear down really hard.*

I tossed the papers in the receptacle outside the elevator, then walked down the corridor of the old Hackard Building to my office, and opened the door.

No day can be all bad. This one blossomed like a rose in sunlight because Velda was bent over filing papers in the lower drawer of a file cabinet with her back toward me, standing with that stiff-kneed dancer's stance, feet together, and no woman in the world has legs like she has. Those calves and thighs, and the lush globes they led to, came from an era when women were fully-fleshed and the posture she was maintaining would be damn near obscene if it weren't unintentional. And what this big luscious brunette could do to a simple white silk blouse, a black pencil skirt and nylons was sheer sexual alchemy.

She heard me, glanced around and stood up quickly, almost having the decency to blush. Almost.

I said, "Didn't anybody ever warn you about picking up the soap in the shower, doll?"

"A guy could knock," she said.

"And then a guy would miss the sweetest surprises." I pushed the door shut. "Besides, I'm a true connoisseur of the female form."

"I noticed."

"I think of it as living erotic art."

Her mouth pursed into an amused kiss. "Do you now?"

I tossed my hat on her desk, slung my hip on the edge and picked up my mail. "Anything come in?"

Velda tugged her skirt down, got back behind her desk and said, "A couple of bills, two checks and a referral from the Smith-Torrence Agency."

"Referral, huh?"

"It's in that stack there."

I sorted the envelopes and fingered out the agency one. "What's with Smitty, anyway, calling me in? He knows I don't handle auditing cases."

"Well, read it and see."

I yanked out the letter and glanced at it. "Hell, it's six pages long and starts with his latest fishing trip. I wouldn't want to read about my own fishing trip. Brief me."

Velda reached out, took the letter and selected the last page. "Smith-Torrence has a request for the kind of thing *they* don't handle. Seems one Leif Borensen has security needs."

Sitting perched where I'd been when Woodcock came in yesterday, I glanced back at her and asked, "Where do I know that name from?"

"You got me," she said with a shrug. "I never heard it before, and haven't had time to run a check."

"Don't bother. If I decide to take this, Smitty will fill me in. Just give me the basics, baby."

She shrugged again. "Borensen's somebody with money who's getting married. He wants security in attendance at his fiancée's bridal shower. It's at the Waldorf."

I made a face. "If it's a female shindig, you should take the gig."

Velda shrugged again. "Smitty says he needs a security man. I'd never pass the physical."

"Truer words."

She flipped a hand. "Anyway, if we're talking high society, the gifts could be worth a small fortune and the gals in attendance might be swimming in jewelry, and not the paste variety. My guess is that we should both be working it."

Like I said, Velda was no mere secretary. She was a full partner in this firm. Some day I'd make her a full partner period.

I swiftly scanned the paragraphs she indicated and let out a snort of disgust. "Why pass this on to me? If this guy Borensen wants to make a show of it, he'll want uniformed guards. Burns or Pinkerton make those scenes. I'll look like a damn clown in that circle."

She shook her head and grinned at me. "Quit being touchy about your obvious lack of class. If you'd read the letter, you'd see that the client doesn't want to be ostentatious. He just wants somebody handy to avoid pilfering by the hotel staff and in the unlikely event of a robbery. Nothing you haven't done before."

I said, "Back when I was scratching out a living, maybe."

"You're not all that rich yet."

"Balls."

"See what I mean about your lack of class? Anyway, Smitty's doing you a favor." She nodded toward the bullet hole in the wall behind her, and gestured toward the faint red smear across the way, made by Woodcock's insides. "Your recent surge of publicity gives you a stigma that may be off-putting to a certain breed of client."

"Where would I be," I said, "without you to cut me down to size."

Her smile had something impish in it. "I'm the only person in town who would have taken a bet that you could have wiped that Woodcock character out the way you did—a guy with a gun in his hand, facing you down like that." Her eyes grew grave. "Listen, Mike, I'm sorry about…"

I swung around so I was sitting on the side edge of the desk now and rested my left hand against the top so I could lean in and face her. "Forget it, kitten."

"I put you in that spot. I can't *believe* I left that door unlocked when I left."

"Your girl friend had a doctor's appointment and needed your support. You were distracted, and you're human. I said forget it and I mean forget it."

She touched my hand. "I appreciate that, Mike. I'm supposed to be as professional as you are, and—"

"Honey, stop. How did that come out, anyway? With your friend, Karen?"

Her big brown eyes were pearled with tears; her lush, red-lipsticked mouth went crinkly with a smile. "It was benign. She's all in the clear."

"That's great. That's fantastic to hear."

The emotional moment over, Velda smirked up at me. "I don't suppose you're going to tell me how this played out."

"I should be dead," I admitted. "He was a contract man with a long list of kills. Somebody paid him to lay me out, but he got chatty and gave me a window."

I told her the rest of the story, including what Pat had come up with on Mr. Woodcock, formerly of Chicago, formerly not shot to shit.

When I finished, her brow creased with suspicion and she said, "Mike—are you into something I don't know about?"

I shook my head.

Her eyes narrowed. "Then… any ideas what this could be?"

"Not a one."

"You wouldn't kid a girl."

"Sure I would. But I'm not."

She gave me a humorless smile. "Well, you don't seem very damn worked up about it."

"That's close to what Pat said." I picked a loose cigarette from my coat pocket and held a match to it.

"I wish you hadn't started that up again," she said with a mild frown.

"What, smoking? You think *this* is what's gonna kill Mike Hammer? You shouldn't have told me I was getting a paunch. These coffin nails are my diet pills."

"It does seem like it helped fake out that hitman. A glass ashtray in the head can daze a person."

"Damn straight." I blew a stream of smoke toward the ceiling, then said, "A lot of guys would pay to have me dead sooner than cigs can make me that way, kiddo. Some I helped send up might be out by now and getting the loot together to pay for the job.

A relative of somebody I knocked off could feel it's his duty to take care of me before he kicked his own pail over. Maybe it's a longtime grudge deal. Hell, I don't know and I don't give much of a damn. I'm no kid any more, and if there's any survival pattern needed here, I picked up on it a long time ago. This is a pretty stinking goddamn world when you consider our end of the business, but if somebody wants to pay to bump me, then he'd better have one piss-pot of money to put on the line."

She was slowly shaking her head. "You're getting jaded, Mike."

"No. Just a seasoned professional, sugar."

"You don't fool me."

"What do you mean?"

She grinned at me. "You don't give much of a damn, huh? You aren't going to find out who hired this? You're not going to settle the score? What great man was it that said, 'Balls?'" She shook her head some more and the sleek black locks danced. "You and that damn .45 of yours."

"Pat said something like that, too."

"When are you going to grow up," she asked, just a little cross, "and stop playing cops and robbers?"

"I thought it was cowboys and Indians."

"Either way, what will you be when you finally grow up?"

"The master. And you can be the mistress."

"I'm that already."

"Then why do you blush when I see those legs of yours climbing all the way to heaven?"

Her chin came up. "Because 'mistress' is a thankless role. Because a marriage license isn't expensive."

"Why buy a cow when milk's so cheap?"

"Sweet talker. If you knew what I was saving for you, for the really *big* night? You wouldn't be so damn vulgar."

"Tell me. Maybe I'll spring for that license."

She rose from the chair and came up into my arms, that big, lovely woman with the startling pageboy hair that shimmered in crazy black-chestnut colors, and let me feel all of her against me and then she whispered in my ear what she had in mind for me, some day.

Some night.

I cocked my head back. "Now who's being vulgar?"

"I am," she said. "But it takes real bait to land a big fish."

Then she did that thing with her mouth when she kissed me, like she was slowly, sensuously trying to twist my lips off my puss, that left me feeling turned inside out.

"Let's go in my office," I said.

"Dictation?"

"Something like that."

"This time I'll lock that door...."

Marion Coulter Smith was an ex-arson squad cop who would likely belt you in the mouth if you called him by his first name.

Fifteen years ago he retired and teamed up with Jules Torrence, a lawyer with a C.P.A. certificate, and formed an investigative firm specializing in industrial accounts with offices in one of the high-end steel-and-glass mausoleums on Sixth Avenue in the heart of the computer district.

It had taken age and business demands to tie Smitty to a desk, and pour him into a three-hundred-dollar suit; but any excuse was good enough to get him in a bull session about the old days or fire up his eyes when the topic got around to crime.

The balding bulldog kept popping open cans of beer from a little fridge in the corner and passing them across his desk to keep me placated if not plastered while I detailed the shoot-out in my office, and the squirming dance the politicians wound up doing, to keep me cooled down enough not to throw any heat back at them.

When I finished, he said, "Damn, you young guys have all the luck. I haven't had *that* kind of fun in I can't remember when."

I about snorted Blue Ribbon out my nose. "Fun? Come off it, Smitty—when the bad guys zero in that close, it's no fun at all."

"Bullshit, Mike. You can't tell me you didn't enjoy it."

"Killing a guy."

"That's what I said."

"What makes you think so?"

Broad shoulders on a hard body gone somewhat flabby shrugged elaborately. "It's just that you have no conscience... anyway, not that the rest of us could notice."

"Don't kid yourself," I said. "I got a conscience like anybody else."

"Maybe you got a conscience," he said, with a tilt of his head, "but not like anybody else. How many people have you shot, anyway?"

"Shot and killed, or just shot?"

"Just the fatalities, man."

I waved that off. "Enough."

"See? A man with a conscience would know the number. How many women have you been with?"

I grinned at him. "*Not* enough."

We both laughed at that.

Then I put my smile away and said, "Anybody I took down had it coming, Smitty. People think I'm some kind of vigilante or executioner or some damn thing. But it's always been a matter of survival with me."

Smitty's eyes glinted. "Your style of survival, Mike, isn't the usual kind. Maybe that's what makes cops tick—them and firemen and other people in high-risk professions. Anybody can survive if they want to hide out in a cave all the time, never stick their nose out, let alone their neck. It takes a different breed to jump into an occupation that deliberately lowers the survival rate."

"Maybe."

"Maybe hell." His finger pointed at me past the beer can in his mitt. "When a guy goes looking for trouble, he can always find it. Put yourself in the trouble spots, and it will find you."

"Is that right."

"It's right. Not just anybody can pull the trigger, even when the gun's loaded and their life is in danger. But with you, it's instinctive. And you even get a kick out of it. A real charge."

I took a long pull of the beer. "Quit psychoanalyzing me, Marion. It's not your specialty."

Me razzing him with his name only made him grin broader.

"Maybe I'm just envying you from behind this desk." He swigged at his beer. "Anyway, society needs your type around. I'd just like to know why, when you seem well past your... youthful indiscretions, shall we say? Why somebody ups and puts out a contract on you."

"You got me, brother."

He was studying me through eyes set in pouches of fat. "Well, if *you* don't know why, then there's something awfully off-kilter about the notion. If getting you out of the way were a necessity, I could see it. But if somebody is playing a game, even if it's a game of some old grudge, they're taking a long chance… You sure you don't have anything big shaking?"

I finished the beer, put the empty on the desk and waved off another he was trying to force on me. "Maybe it was just mistaken identity."

"Guy stakes your office out for weeks and… oh. You're just rattling my chain."

"Something like that. You don't have to look so damn pleased that somebody tried to knock me off."

The bulldog puss split in a smile. "Why not? You make interesting entertainment for us put-out-to-pasture types. Anyway, as far as psychology goes, I've often wondered about you guys with no consciences."

"How about entertaining *me*?" I asked. "With this referral?" I tossed the letter he had sent me on the blotter in front of him. "And you can skip the fishing trip."

Smitty leaned back in his chair, grinned, shrugged, and said, "Good pay, easy work. We're just not set up for it. Play watchdog for an afternoon and get a grand for your trouble."

"For a grand," I said, sitting forward, "you can't cover the place yourself?"

He gave me a humorless grunt. "Ha. With the dough we make, that'd be a tax liability. Anyway, I could have shoved it off on one of our own legmen, but we don't like 'em moonlighting when we pay their salaries… and besides, I thought it would be a hoot having you drop around for a briefing. A live one like you perks things up, once in a while." He paused and fingered a cigar out of the silver humidor on the window sill behind him. "So, Mike? Want the job?"

"Not particularly, but I could use the grand. What's the pitch?"

Smitty bit off the end of the cigar, lit it and coughed on the fumes he sucked in. "Leif Borensen. Ever hear of him?"

I frowned in thought. "It's a familiar name somehow. Did I see it on the end credits of a TV show as a producer or something?"

"Bingo. He's a local boy who went to L.A. and made good, twenty years or so ago. He was a lucky land speculator out there, picked up shares in several corporations on trading deals and one of them was a supposedly defunct production company. He got hold of some sharp production people who put it back on its feet and started making some cheap pictures—you know, monsters, juvies, sci-fi—and then made half-hour syndicated series for TV. He's not exactly a Zanuck, more a one-man studio, but he's successful enough… and most important, he pays his bills."

"Sounds like he's used your agency before."

Smitty nodded. "We checked out personnel and company records for him on four different projects when he bought up corporations. He wasn't aware we don't handle personal stuff, like this bridal shower gig, so he just put his request through this office again."

"Maybe he won't dig you not handling it personally."

"Client's already okayed our recommendation," Smitty said with a dismissive wave.

He stopped, grinned again, rolled over to the little fridge on his swivel chair and came back opening another beer for himself.

"In fact, Mike, he seemed pleased. He's heard of you. Actually, you're more in line with what he wants. A real gunslinger type."

"Nuts."

"Oh, I'm serious, Mike my boy. That bash for his fiancée will be strictly society stuff. All the jewels will be out. You'll be sitting on top of enough silver to start your own mint, and if your luck holds, maybe it'll attract a nice stupid burglar you can knock off and get your thrills and some more headlines… and then you can come in here and tell me all about it. You know I like those gory details." His belly shook in a silent laugh.

I was starting to get pissed off. He'd gone over the line with this crap. There was no humor in my voice when I said, "Cut that shit out, Smitty."

"Now don't tell me you're getting sensitive at this late date, Mike." He pulled open his desk drawer, slid out a single printed form and handed it across to me. "Here's the details. Just to show you what kind of friend I am… even if I do get a kick out of needling you… I didn't deduct any percentage for the initial contact. Your check will come directly from the client."

I read the sheet, folded it, stuck it in my pocket and stood up.

"Thanks," I said. I'd gotten kind of irritated, but he deserved that much.

His grin came back through the cigar smoke. "No thanks

necessary, Mike. The talk was worth it. I keep trying to figure out you guys with no consciences. It's an interesting gambit."

I slapped my hat on and walked to the door. There was a mirror beside it and I caught my eyes in the reflection. The coldness in their gray-blue disturbed even me.

Then I turned to him. "So how many did *you* shoot, back in your day, Smitty?"

There was no laugh in his face and the fire in his eyes dulled to a small, dying glow. He said nothing, but I wasn't going to leave until he answered me.

The fire went out entirely and he said softly, "Too many."

CHAPTER THREE

A cold front was sticking its tongue out at New York, tasting the edges of it, and—not liking what it found—spitting it back in a short, chilly blast. The rush-hour crowd made shoulder-brushing two-lane traffic on the sidewalks, and the usual batch of arm-wavers were jostling each other in the streets trying to flag down cabs at the worst possible time.

I said the hell with it and crossed Sixth Avenue with the light and headed east back to my apartment, playing city safari until I got past Park Avenue. Manhattan was quite a jungle and not that different from the one in Africa. Every time one faction got out of hand and threatened to destroy the terrain, the game wardens moved in, rounded them up, and moved them to someone else's domain. In Africa it was various species of animals. In New York it was just one lousy species—people—though with its various sub-species. For instance, now that the cops had confined the whores to the side streets, the girls were waving at you out of the windows, like Amsterdam but without the sexy mood lighting.

When I reached Lexington, I turned north to pick up an evening paper at Billy Batson's newsstand. Billy is one of the world's larger little people—he was the tallest of the Singer Midgets, making him easy to spot in *The Wizard of Oz*—and twenty years ago or so, he'd invested ten years of decent show biz money into a newsstand at a prime spot. His real last name I never knew, but since his stand had always sported the best array of funny books on any Manhattan street corner, he got tagged with the name of Captain Marvel's alter ego, newsboy Billy Batson.

Now Captain Marvel was gone, sued out of existence by the Superman crowd, while Billy Batson was still here, and so was a colorful display of comic books dominated by newcomers like *Spider-Man* and *The Fantastic Four*. Billy was a sharp, streetwise character in a plaid golf cap, a padded quilt jacket, black flannel trousers, and Keds. He spotted me when I first turned the corner and had my paper ready.

"How you hangin', Mike?"

"By the thumbs, like the guys on the radio say. How about you, Billy?"

He tossed a hand. "Don't do no good complainin'. Hey, man, that was some lousy picture of you in the *News* this morning."

"What can I say? My make-up man had the day off."

He grunted a laugh, made some change for a customer and turned back to me. "That story stunk worse than the pic. A load of crap, if my sniffer's still workin' right."

"One man's load of crap is another's official police version."

"Come off it, Mike. Who they tryin' to kid? A hold-up guy in *your* office building? If they said he was a sex pervert and going after Velda, I mighta gone for it. But busting into a private cop's office, for money he wouldn't keep there, even if he had any? Weak, man, real weak."

"Don't look to get original fiction out of homicide cops, Billy. They're not trained that way, and they got limited imaginations."

He worked the fig leaf of his coin changer for another customer. "So lay the real spiel on me, man. I ain't the general public."

"Simple," I said. "The guy tried to tap me out."

"Somebody with a grudge?"

"Somebody paid a wad of dough to have the deed done."

Billy gave me an incredulous look that ended in a laugh. "A hitman… for Mike Hammer?"

"Why not?"

"Well, hell's bells, Mike… it's like tryin' to assassinate the Abominable Snowman."

"Thanks a bunch."

"Yeah, well, look what it got the guy. Anyway, that this-gun-for-hire stuff comes high. What did you ever do to deserve that kind of fancy treatment?"

"I wish I knew."

He eyed me suspiciously. "You ain't been messin' around with some other guy's broad, have you?"

Little Billy had a big yen for Velda, and me cheating on her would just about make a hit justifiable in his mind.

"Nobody's broad but my own," I assured him.

"Big beautiful Velda."

"Big beautiful Velda."

He made change again for a customer buying two papers, something he could do in his sleep. "Maybe you're steppin' on the wrong toes. Mob guys, maybe. I remember when you was pretty good at that."

"I haven't rated more than a frown from that bunch or anybody else for a good three years. Those headlines this morning were the first in a long damn time. You know that, Billy."

His wrinkled puss wrinkled some more. "Then your past is catching up to you, my friend. Maybe somebody you goosed once upon a time finally got enough loot together to get you splashed but good."

"Yeah? At this rate they'll run out of money fast."

Billy shrugged and grunted another laugh, a humorless one. "One killing does not necessarily a bankruptcy make, old buddy."

"Sounds like you've been reading again," I said. "Stick to the funny books."

He ignored that, sold another paper, then said, "If you rated a contract, they'll try again, you know."

"Should make for an interesting autumn," I told him. "How are you doing with that identification? Getting anywhere?"

Just shy of a month ago, a hit-and-run driver had killed a customer strolling away from this newsstand. Billy was the only witness who got a good look at the driver.

Billy shrugged, shaking his head, unconcerned. "My eyes are shot from goin' through mug books lookin' at ugly faces. Twice last week they took me downtown for a line-up, but it didn't do no good. The guy I saw wasn't one of those slobs. I keep tellin' 'em. He was class, I could see that easy."

"Too bad nobody got the license plate. That the victim was a regular of yours makes it personal, I bet."

"Oh yeah, and it's a damn shame. Dick Blazen. Did you know him, Mike?"

"Naw. Papers said he was some kind of freelance PR guy."

Billy nodded. "Been around forever. Retired last year. Then retired into that gutter over there and after that a box in the ground. How I would love to help nail the bastard who made road refuse outa that sweet old bird."

I lifted a shoulder and put it back down. "The cops do all right on that kind of thing. They'll come up with the right guy for you to ID yet."

"Hope so." He passed out a couple more papers, taking correct change, then asked, "What's up for tonight? Got a hot date with that doll of yours?"

I shrugged. "Not exactly a date. Velda and I are going to put our heads together over dinner. See if we can come up with somebody who doesn't love me."

"That'll be swell for your appetites." He pointed a stubby finger at me. "You just keep that chick out of the line of fire, Mike. Hear me?"

I stuck my paper under my arm and winked. "I try, kid, I try. But she's damn near as trigger-happy as I am."

That got a smile out of the crinkly face, and he waved as I walked off.

When I finished getting dressed, I popped open a cold can of beer and pulled the duplicate hot file out of the closet's top shelf, stuck behind hats and gloves and scarves.

It was something an old cop had started me doing a long time ago, keeping track of anyone and anything that might want to come back on me, and to do so in duplicate—a set for the office, another at home. The little metal file held my history in the P.I. racket, and a blood-drenched history it was.

Sending me to the boneyard had been tried before and never worked, because each time had been a personal effort and I had been a little smarter and a lot faster and death cures any further trying.

But this time a third party had been involved. A professional killer. That made it a different kind of game, a big all-star game and the other side had the advantage of invisibility, and nobody would be calling foul.

Twice, I went through the card file, going back a full five years; but the only ones who could have had a grudge big enough to kill me over had been dead a long time, or were serving life sentences with no parole. Finally I yanked out two of the cards, copied the information down on my notepad, then slipped the cards back in place. There was always the possibility of a late blooming vendetta, and if one had blossomed, it might well have come from the family or friends of the pair I had selected. It wouldn't take long to check out.

Before I left I reloaded the .45 with high velocity hollow points and slid it into the shoulder harness. It made one hell of a mean weapon, but if anybody was going to come up against me, I wanted all the odds I could get going my way. Just being tipped by one of those slugs could spin a damn horse around, and a full center shot would make a pretty disgusting picture.

Like the one friend Woodcock left behind him on my office wall.

I caught myself in the mirror just before I left. Other than my morning shave, looking at my reflection was something I didn't do much any more, because I didn't like what was there. I'd always been ugly but now I was getting older, and it didn't help. You start counting all the times you've been to the well and know that it had to stop sometime. Time has a way of slowing you down, and making you careless, and when you look at your own face, knowing what it has seen, you wonder how you even have the ability to smile at all any more.

Then I remembered Woodcock in my office and the mechanics of every calculated, seemingly casual move I had made to finally put him down, and let a cold grin split my lips, because expertise and a high survival factor still had the edge on time.

I jammed on my hat, climbed inside my trench-style raincoat and let myself out the door, my hand tucked inside my coat and suit jacket like I was doing a Napoleon routine. The hallway was empty.

The elevator took me down to the basement and I went out the back door and picked up a cab on the street behind the building. It had been a long time since I had to pull any of this garbage, but it had been a long time since anybody had tried to rub me out, too.

The archaic sound of that made me remember just how long I had been around and that such things had been going on around me.

Somehow, I didn't get the charge out of it that I used to. But I would need to get my head in the game or have it get blown the hell off.

* * *

At the venerable Blue Ribbon Restaurant on West Forty-fourth, Velda and I sat in the bar at our usual corner table in a niche overseen by celebrity photos, a good number of whom seemed to be eavesdropping. I'd had the knockwurst plate, Velda a big shrimp salad, and now she was having a Manhattan while I took care of a Four Roses and ginger. She seemed so very businesslike in her gray tailored suit, yet still made every other female in the place look sick.

We'd skipped the business talk during the meal, but now I handed her the two slips of paper with the hot-file leads.

"I'll look into them," she said, giving the notes a quick advance scan before slipping them into her purse.

I frowned at her little black leather shoulder-strap number. "Are you packing the .32?"

The big brown eyes met my concerned stare coolly. "What do you think? If the next guy that tries for you isn't a sharp shooter, *I* could take the slug. If you'll excuse me sounding so sentimental."

I didn't like having her in this at all, but I knew better than suggesting she get out.

"We've had it quiet for a few years," I said. "The mob guys are mostly new faces, and some of them are grateful to me for getting rid of their old bosses and giving them a path to the good life."

She was nodding. "I agree. Everybody's first thought is that the list of those who want rid of Mike Hammer has to be a long one. But between the dead and the incarcerated, you don't have that many enemies walking around at the moment."

"Those two leads I gave you are family members who just might be rough enough to go for the revenge angle. Listen, besides the one in your purse, how about re-upping the old blade in the thigh-sheath gimmick?"

"And ruin my fashionable lines? Not on your life. If you'll excuse the expression."

I sipped my drink. I knew this was a hopeless fight.

I said, "You have a chance to look into our prospective client?"

"Leif Borensen? No. But I did better than that." She looked past me with a smile, and pointed a red-nailed finger. "I arranged for somebody in the know to drop by after dinner."

I glanced at the approaching figure, just another nobody at a glance, a man of average size in glasses and business suit, his face graced by a receding crew cut, but in reality one of America's most popular, powerful syndicated columnists.

Then I was on my feet grinning and we were shaking hands, Hy Gardner and me.

"What brings you back to town?" I demanded cheerfully. "Seems like you just left."

He shrugged and took a chair between us. "Just because the *Trib* is dead doesn't mean my column isn't alive and well. A couple of Broadway musicals are opening this week, and I'm here to cover them."

"Where's Marilyn?" Velda asked.

Marilyn had been Hy's secretary till they married a decade or so ago.

"She's too smart to head north this time of year," Hy said. "I forgot how damn gray this city is! Marilyn's back in Florida where the sun is shining and the water is blue."

Unbidden, head bartender George arrived to bring Hy a bourbon on the rocks. The two old friends exchanged a smile that said more than words, and George vanished.

Velda explained to me, "Hy called this afternoon, to tell you he was in town, and I did what you would have done."

I grinned. "Gave him a job." My eyes met the sly, sleepy ones behind the glasses. "So what can you tell me about Leif Borensen?"

He gave me the kind of casual shrug that always preceded his most elaborate briefings. "He's a big, blond, good-looking guy, kind of a Forrest Tucker or Sonny Tufts type. Gals love him and the feeling's mutual. There are no smudges on his personal behavior. He was drafted during the Korean War, put his time in and was given an honorable discharge. Started out as an actor here in town. Came to the Apple from the Midwest and started landing secondary roles in plays and early TV. He even made it into my column a couple of times."

"Anything notable?"

Hy shook his head. "Played a corpse on *Climax* who got to his feet too soon and walked out of frame. That got him some attention. The wrong kind, maybe... but at least I spelled his name right."

"So this was, what? Twenty years ago?"

"Around then. There wasn't a lot of call for walking corpses on TV, and his looks didn't make up for a stilted delivery. He was landing stage parts based on his strong jaw and muscular physique, but he was strictly straight and lost his appeal with certain casting directors."

"So the show business background explains why he headed to Hollywood."

Hy nodded. "But he wasn't getting cast out there much, either. Second cop from the left, third Indian from the right. He was barely scrounging out an existence when a rich aunt died and left him some dough and he started taking fliers in real estate. There were still bargains to be had in those days, and he did well. A production company he acquired as an offshoot of one land deal or another turned him into a producer, and for fifteen years, give or take, he's been churning out drive-in fodder and doing well at it. You know, *The Monster That Ate Cleveland*, *I Was a Teenage Zombie*. Also some of those half-hour syndicated jobs that come on in the non-network slots before the news and after the *Tonight Show*. Private eye junk, mostly."

Velda smiled at that.

I said, "And now he's back in the big town."

Hy sipped bourbon and nodded again. "I hear he's got the bug to be a *real* producer. The real Broadway deal. His fiancée, Gwen Foster... have you heard of her?"

"No," I said.

Velda touched my sleeve. "Sure you have, Mike. She had one of the leads in that *Dames at Sea* revival we saw last year."

"Too many dames to keep track of in that," I said with a shrug. "Is she any good, Hy?"

"Very good. Beautiful singing voice, nice comedic touch, and a real stunner. She could go far. She has the genes for it."

At first I thought he said "jeans," but then I got the drift. I snapped my fingers. "Martin Foster. Her father?"

The late Foster had been one of the city's most successful theatrical producers, right in there with David Merrick.

Hy nodded. "But it's not a nepotism situation. She's really got it. And her daddy didn't produce that revival you saw, either."

"Still," I said, skeptical. "Connections."

"No, Mike," Velda said. "She's good. Very good."

"She may be rushing into this marriage," Hy said, eyebrows climbing over his glasses.

I frowned. "How so?"

He asked Velda if she minded if he smoked a cigar; she said she didn't, and he withdrew one of his typical Havana pool cues from an inside pocket like a passport.

"Starting maybe four months ago," Hy said, getting the cigar going, waving out a match, "Borensen and Gwen's father were exploring mounting a new production, a musical version of an old Maxwell Anderson play, *The Star Wagon*. They were courting Johnny Mercer and had him within an inch of a contract. Then, two months ago... and you may remember this from the papers, Mike... Foster shot himself at his Long Island summer home."

"Anything suspicious about it?"

Hy grinned and Velda smirked; they exchanged eye rolls.

"What?" I said.

"It's just that you're so predictable, man," Hy said, and he finished off his bourbon. George was there with another before Hy had set it down.

Velda said, "Mike, the autopsy said Foster was in an advanced stage of lung cancer. He was a who-knows-how-many-packs-a-day smoker. Maybe you should think about that."

"Thanks for the reminder," I said, and got out my Luckies and fired one up. But it only made her smile and shake her head a little.

"When did you take those up again?" Hy asked.

"I needed something to soothe my jangly nerves," I said. "So Borensen and Gwen got to know each other when he and her father were doing business, probably just a friendly, flirtatious bit that turned into something."

"It turned into something, all right," Hy said. "An upcoming wedding. And Martin Foster was a very rich, successful guy, Mike. That bridal shower they want you for will be star-studded and diamond-studded, too."

"What's the inside word on Borensen?"

Hy shrugged again. "They say he's tight with a buck and knows just how to squeeze a nickel. His pictures have made money because he doesn't spend much on them. He racked up his fortune giving talented young guys a break and seasoned old pros much needed work. His TV shows, you've seen 'em, always star washed-up Hollywood guys, with just enough name value left to lend Borensen's productions some credibility."

I grunted a laugh. "That just says he's a good businessman. What about personally?"

"He seems well-liked, as far as that goes. He keeps a low profile. Despite his acting background, he's never given himself a role. His kind of producing hasn't got him much attention anywhere but the Hollywood trades, and maybe those monster magazines the kids read."

"You smell an opportunist, Hy? Is he gold-digging that girl?"

The columnist's smile was small but hugely cynical. "Look,

Mike, Gwen Foster's rich and beautiful and talented. What's not to love? But Borensen's already got plenty of dough. On his own terms, he's a hell of a success. What he *doesn't* have is that glow of show business royalty that the Foster name can bring him."

I blew smoke skyward. "So where is this headed? Maybe he produces a successful Broadway musical with his talented bride, sells the movie rights to a big Hollywood studio, and finagles a producer spot for himself. And suddenly he's climbing."

"It's the American way, Mike," Hy said with a grin.

I shook my head. "If only *I* could find a rich, talented, beautiful woman."

Velda kicked me under the table.

"Well," I said, wincing just a little, "it all sounds vaguely sleazy to me, but we can use the bread. Velda, first thing tomorrow, set up a meeting for me with our esteemed social-climbing producer. I think we'll let him produce a thousand dollars for Hammer Investigations."

CHAPTER FOUR

The apartment building was one of those old stately places on Park Avenue in the East Sixties. Central Park nestled outside of it like a huge countryside estate behind its endless stone fence. From the rows of windows, the park's rolling slopes would make a pretty sight sometimes, traffic flowing through the greenery, people strolling the pathways. After dark it wouldn't seem so pretty any more, but nobody in the stately building would give a damn, because they couldn't see what went on down there anyway, among the lesser classes.

The day had a nice Indian summer feel to it and I'd left my coat and hat behind. I looked very modern, all hatless and decked out in my one Brooks Brothers suit, a nice shade of gray with black flecks.

I told the doorman Mr. Borensen was expecting me and cooled my heels while he confirmed it over the interphone, and when he told me twelve D, I said thanks and trooped across a marble-floored lobby no fancier or larger than a hotel ballroom to a bank of elevators and punched the button.

To supplement Hy filling me in last night, Velda had done a good job this morning of running a further check on our prospective client. It wasn't a necessity, but if there was anything shaky in his background, we'd know what angles needed covering. A source at the LAPD and another at the recently formed Producers Guild of America backed up Hy's briefing and filled in a few blanks.

Apparently the motion picture business had dominated Borensen's time in the sunshine state, but not with the kind of success that really made you somebody in Movieland. He had stayed on the outer fringes of that money game until he lucked into his land development scheme and parlayed his modest inheritance into the kind of loot that could attract more. Add that to his upcoming nuptials to a very rich young woman, and he was ready to go into major production.

Leif Borensen was rich now and there sure as hell wasn't anything wrong with being rich, even if it meant hiring somebody like me to keep the poor people at bay.

The elevator hissed to a stop and I stepped off into that wonderful world where money could rent digs with a huge private foyer complete with running waterfall and a hidden electronic system that announced you to a beautiful blonde who bounced out and asked, "Mr. Hammer?"

She was a stunning, lightly tanned thing in a white ribbed sleeveless sweater and cherry-red slacks with matching wide big-buckled belt and a rather silly-looking, oversize puffy cap. A little slimmer than I like them, but I understood how a guy could overlook that. And she had the kind of delicately feminine features that made Audrey Hepburn look like she just wasn't trying.

Before I could answer, she held out her hand and her red

lipsticked kiss of a mouth said, "I'm Gwen Foster, Mr. Hammer—Mr. Borensen's fiancée."

I took the hand and kept it as long as I could get away with. "Nice to see you, Miss Foster. Of course, I've seen you before."

Light blue, blue-eye-shadowed eyes got big and bright, framed by large individually separated lashes. "Oh?"

"On stage. *Dames at Sea* last year. You made quite an impression."

Okay, it never hurts to butter up the client's wife, even the "almost" variety.

"Very kind of you, Mr. Hammer. Please come in. Leif is waiting for you inside."

Not right inside, though, because she walked me into and through a high-ceilinged foyer bigger than my apartment, with more marble flooring, a crystal chandelier looming, and a staircase at left sweeping up like it was on its way to have Loretta Young come down.

"We're so pleased you've agreed to provide some protection at my shower," she said, leading the way briskly. The red trousers revealed a nicely shaped, full bottom despite her slender frame. Detectives notice these things.

"I haven't actually said yes, Miss Foster. I need to speak to your fiancé first."

She came to an abrupt stop and I almost bumped into her, which would have been fun but embarrassing.

We were in the midst of a hallway that was like an airport runway with an Oriental carpet. Several more chandeliers hovered and the paintings around us in their gilt-edged or sometimes modern frames were an eclectic array, everything from Renoir to Picasso. The baroque furnishings hugging the walls seemed expensively antique.

She faced me and retrieved my hand and held it in two of hers. "Oh, I hope you will say yes to the job. I'm counting on it. I'd be so disappointed if you said no."

Those blue eyes were the color of a waterfall-fed pool that I wouldn't have minded jumping into.

"Are you expecting trouble, Miss Foster?"

Her smile made her peach-blushed apple cheeks go even bigger and her teeth were perfect and white, God and a dentist collaborating beautifully.

"No, not at all. I don't expect a daylight robbery at the Waldorf, for pity sake. Leif seems a little paranoid about that, but… it's just that I've told my girl friends you'll be guarding the festivities, and they are very excited. Especially the older ones."

I winced. "I was going to guess I was a little before your time. You've confirmed it."

Red blush worked its way up under the peach. "No, I'm sorry, so sorry… it's just—they told me some wild things about you. Way-out things. They said when you were a young man… *younger* man… you used to fill the headlines with the most outrageous escapades. Like something out of an old Bogart movie."

I smiled. "All Bogart movies are old, Miss Foster."

Still, that was a kind of nice compliment, a little left-handed but nice. Of course, Bogart never racked up my body count.

She deposited me at a doorway. She had never let go of my hand. Her touch was the damnedest thing—warm and cool at once.

"Leif's just inside," she said.

"Are you joining us?"

"No. I'm a modern girl, but I know when it's man-talk time."

Maybe there was hope for this new generation after all.

But I pressed: "I'm a little surprised you're not going to be part of the meeting, Gwen. And it's Mike."

"Hi Mike. Why's that?"

"Well, why meet at your place, if you're not going to be part of the discussion?"

"Oh. I see. I hope you won't be shocked, but after Daddy's death, I asked Leif to move in here with me, and he said yes."

If she got to know me better, she'd learn I didn't shock quite so easily.

"You know, I knew your father," I said.

The eyes widened again. Were those spaced-apart lashes fake? I didn't care. They made blue sunflowers out of those eyes.

Very interested, she asked, "Were you friends with Daddy?"

"That overstates it. Friendly acquaintances even overstates it. But we each knew who the other was, and if we were in the same place would at least say hello and sometimes chat. Very charming guy. I admire his success. Nice man."

She gave me half a smirk. "Not everyone who did business with Daddy would agree. He gave his stars fits, directors, too. Do you know what Anthony Newley said about Daddy?"

"No."

"'Will Rogers said he never met a man he didn't like. Well, Will Rogers never met Martin Foster.'"

We both laughed a little at that.

"I miss him," she said, letting the sadness show in that lovely face. "At first I was so… so *mad* at him. But he must have been in a lot of pain."

There was nothing to say to that, but, "How are you holding up, Gwen?"

"All I can say is, Leif's been a real boon in all this. I don't know where I'd be, or how I'd have begun to deal with this thing, without him." She gave my hand a final little squeeze. "Now, go on in there, Mike."

She bounced off, the cute red-clad bottom bidding me a friendly goodbye. Half-way down the cavernous hall, she looked back and called out, echoing a little, "Don't worry about getting lost. I'll be back to collect you!"

I went on through into a two-story study, dominated by dark masculine woods, the kind of book-lined affair that needs library ladders on both its floors. One wall was plaster and bookless, though, reserved for a fireplace and framed photos of stage and screen stars and the occasional celebrity politician, all featuring the late Martin Foster in handshake or arm-around-the-shoulder pose. In the midst of this was a big framed Hirschfeld caricature of the departed producer—damn near the size of a movie poster.

The floor was parquet but a good deal of it was taken up by another Oriental carpet, on which perched half a dozen brown-leather easy chairs surrounding a glass-topped coffee table, fairly massive, *Playbill* programs of Foster's many theatrical productions spread out on display within.

But the most impressive thing in the room was a man who had to be Leif Borensen, a big, grinning blond guy looking for all the world as if he had just stepped ashore from a Viking longboat—

if Vikings wore camel-colored cardigans, light pink shirts, gray slacks, and Rolex watches.

He'd heard me come in and left his easy chair by the coffee table to approach with a smile and an outstretched paw. We shook, and neither of us showed off, and he introduced himself and gestured me to one of the easy chairs.

"Can I get you something to drink, Mr. Hammer?"

"I wouldn't turn my nose up at a rye and ginger."

"Rocks?"

"Why not?"

At a nearby bar cart, he built that and something for himself as well, and sat across from me, that glassed-in array of his late father-in-law's theatrical triumphs between us.

"You live up to your billing, Mr. Hammer."

"Do I?"

He gestured with his tumbler of what appeared to be Scotch. "You're big and look mean as hell. I'd cast you in one of my TV shows if I didn't think you'd scare the women and children."

I smiled at that. "Call me if a bad guy role opens up. Now what's this about a thousand dollars?"

He sipped the apparent Scotch. Single malt, no doubt. I wondered if it was older than his fiancée. *He* certainly was— fifty, easily, though his face wasn't as lined as you'd think. Plastic surgery perhaps, or maybe he didn't use his face much.

"I have to admit," he said, smiling mostly with his eyes and confirming my latter notion, "that I was tickled when Smith-Torrence suggested you as a referral."

"Oh?"

He nodded and set the drink down on a coaster on a little mahogany table between him and the next chair. "I admit to being a fan. You may not know this, but I was a working actor… or anyway, I worked occasionally… back in your heyday in the early '50s."

"Is that right?"

"Am I irritating you?"

"No. I always look and sound like this."

He shook his head, chuckled. "Well, I used to get a real kick out of it. Years later, I would tell the writers on my private eye shows, 'Do a little research on that Mike Hammer in New York. Then you'll know what a *real* tough private eye is really like.'"

"Nobody ever accused me of that before."

He sipped Scotch, then gave me a concerned look. "What about this recent incident? Killing a burglar in your building?"

"Just looking after my interests," I said with a shrug.

Everybody didn't need to know a hitman was gunning for me. That might discourage business.

"So," I said, changing the subject, "I'm who you think is right for a bridal shower security job? Sounds a little like overkill to me."

He waved a hand like a bored magician. "I'll understand if you want to take a pass, Mr. Hammer. This might be beneath you."

"Yeah, it might be," I said, "but that grand you mentioned to Smitty is just about eye level."

He grinned with his whole face this time, and some lines came out of hiding. "It'll be an afternoon affair, starting at four and going till six-thirty, this coming Friday."

This was Tuesday. "I was going to ask you about that. Why such short notice?"

"The invites have been out for two weeks, but it was only after I got to thinking that I realized having some security makes a lot of sense. You see, we're getting married in Hawaii at the end of the month, no family, with just a handful of friends we're flying out with us. Just a romantic beach-side ceremony with lots of flowers and a luau after."

I was ahead of him. "So this shower takes the place of a wedding reception."

"Right. I have almost no friends in Manhattan any more, but of course Gwen does, and that means the gift table will be piled with treasures."

"Understood."

"I'd want you there at three, Mr. Hammer, just to get a handle on things. It's at the Waldorf. I forget the suite number—I'll get it to you."

"How many guests?"

"Fifty very wealthy women. We'll have some high-end entertainment, too. It's essentially a cocktail party."

"Do you expect trouble?"

"Not at all. But between the gifts and what those women will drape themselves with… could make a thief's haul worth a couple of hundred thousand."

I worked up a whistle.

"And a hold-up man with a gun," Borensen said, eyebrows raised, "wouldn't have much trouble intimidating a room full of females."

Maybe, but not all females were alike.

I said, "I'm bringing my second-in-command along."

"Miss Sterling? Velda?"

"That's right. You've done your research."

He smiled, shrugged. "She used to make the papers, too. Yes, I think that would be fine. I can bump the fee to $1500, if you like."

"Bump away."

He wrote me out a $750 check on the spot as a retainer.

I held the check in my fingertips and let the ink dry. "Do I need to rent a tux?"

"No. Just your best business suit."

I gestured to myself. "This is it. Suitable?"

"A suitable suit, Mr. Hammer. Not to worry."

He rose. I was in the process of being dismissed.

I got up, glancing around. "Cozy little place you have here."

He laughed sadly as he came around to walk me out. "Yes, Martin was a hell of a showman. And he didn't live small. He was only married once, though—did you know that?"

"I guess I didn't."

"Kind of remarkable, considering the, uh, opportunities a man like him would have. Gwen's mother was in the chorus line of one of Martin's first musicals. She had Gwen's looks but not her talent. Still, she grew into the role of a society woman, as the Foster fame grew."

The Foster bankroll, too.

"I heard you were in the process of mounting a new musical yourself," I said, "when Foster took his life."

He visibly paled. "Terrible thing. Awful tragedy. I had no idea Martin was in such… misery. He'd kept his cancer from us entirely. I haven't smoked for years, and I'm glad of it."

"Me, too, only recently I picked it back up again."

"Well, stop, Mr. Hammer, if you don't mind a little friendly advice. And, yes, I returned to the scene of my initial failure in show business in search of the redemption that can only be brought by success."

That had come out of nowhere, and sounded like a line he'd worked up for the newspapers.

I asked, "Is it shelved now, the project?"

"Temporarily. But I have Johnny Mercer on board for the music, and I've got Larry Gelbart on the hook for the book—he wrote *A Funny Thing Happened on the Way to the Forum*."

"I saw that. Some good laughs. Lots of pretty girls. Do that again."

He chuckled. "I'll try. I *can* guarantee you one thing."

"Which is?"

He sipped his Scotch. "We'll have a hell of a fantastic leading lady."

As promised, Gwen was there in her silly red puffy hat and nicely snug jeans, waiting to see me back out. She and Borensen shared a quick kiss before he disappeared back into the study. Then she batted the big blue eyes at me as she took my arm.

"So, Mike. What do you think of my man?"

"He's well-preserved."

She smiled smirkily. "You don't approve of a girl in her twenties marrying a man in his fifties?"

"Maybe you should consider a younger man. I'm in my thirties, for example. And will be for another month."

That got a musical laugh from her.

Soon we were down the wide endless corridor and through

the marble-floored foyer and at the door.

"Seriously," she said, "what's your impression of Leif? I imagine, in your business, you have to be a really good judge of character."

"I liked him fine," I said. "And I just love his retainer."

Outside the apartment building, I flagged a Yellow Cab and opened the back door, leaning in. I gave the cabbie the address of the Blue Ribbon, where I was meeting Velda and Hy in half an hour for a post-game report. My driver was a friendly black guy who automatically craned around to give me a smile.

I was half-way through my sentence when dampness spattered my face and tiny stinging shards flecked my cheeks while something metallic hit my chest, not enough to break the skin, just a thump.

As the rifle's crack reached my ears, I had a flash of the bloody irregular hole the size of a quarter in the cabbie's forehead before he fell back over the seat onto the rider's side, the smile still there.

My face was splashed with blood and my cheeks nicked by skull fragments and my chest hurting just a little from the thump of a slowed-down bullet, its velocity cut into harmlessness by travelling through all that bone.

Scrambling, I backed out of the cab crouching onto the sidewalk, the vehicle between me and the shooter, if he was still in position, and I yanked the .45 from under my arm and clicked off the safety. The sidewalks weren't crowded in a high-class neighborhood like this, but an old gal walking two poodles started screaming and a few other pedestrians did, too. Whether they'd heard the shot and were reacting to that or just saw my scarlet splattered face, I had no idea.

I did know who the target was here, and it wasn't the smiling cabbie. Somebody with a rifle had propped himself behind and on the edge of the Central Park wall opposite and taken a tricky shot that would have hit home if that friendly cabbie hadn't suddenly turned to make human contact with me.

I duck-walked around the cab and into the street, the snout of the .45 angled up. Traffic was unaware of the gunshot and kept moving, and was fairly light anyway and not fast either, so I was able to stay low and weave between cars, getting some wide eyes and a few squealing brakes from drivers when they saw a wild-eyed bloody-faced guy in a well-tailored business suit on the prowl with a big automatic in his mitt.

I could already see that no shooter was in place now along the thick stone wall with its touches of green in crevices and overhanging trees spotted along.

Hell—could he have taken his shot from one of these trees?

No, that was stupid. But unless he was a giant, he'd used something to get up over the five-foot high, foot-thick barrier, and take his shot.

I was across the pavement now, still staying low, and onto the wide, tree-shaded brick walkway. What few pedestrians had been around were gone now. Very little impresses New Yorkers, but gunfire gets their attention and summons respect.

I cut left to jump up and grab a low-hanging branch and pulled myself up and over the wall, skirting its pyramidal top, dropping to the grass, landing fairly light, and again keeping low. To my right as I faced the park was a bench against the wall, either a providential aid for my would-be assassin or something he'd moved into place, likely ahead of time. A spent cartridge winked sunlight at me from the grass. I didn't take time to pick it up.

No one suspicious-looking or otherwise was in sight near that bench, but to my left a man was walking very quickly away—a man wearing a gray topcoat unnecessary on this unseasonably balmy day. No one seemed to be in this part of the park right now, possibly because Manhattanites out strolling through it knew a gunshot when they heard it. They were tucked behind trees or had hit the dirt behind bushes.

The man in the topcoat was likely heading toward the exit/ entrance at Fifth Avenue at Sixtieth. I felt confident this was my would-be assassin, but maybe not confident enough to shoot him.

That kind of mistake was hard to live down.

And anyway, I needed him alive for a conversation. That friendly cabbie deserved better, but I needed not to shoot this prick. *Somebody had hired him and I would find out who.* Gun in hand, upright, I ran hard now, cutting the distance quickly.

When I was within fifty feet of him, I yelled, "Stop or I'll shoot!"

He kept moving, glancing back at me. He wore sunglasses, the orange tactical variety, on a bland oval face. *He was the shooter, all right.* White guy, medium height, in that gray topcoat, hatless, short black hair, another face in the crowd like my late pal Woodcock.

I fired a shot into the ground—fire it in the air and a slug might come down and clip somebody—and the roar of it was like a lion was loose from the park zoo.

"*I changed my mind!*" I yelled. And I stopped running. I aimed the .45 in a two-handed grip, my feet apart, firing-range style. "*Please* don't *stop!*"

But he did stop, swinging around and dropping to one knee—he, too, was in a firing-range stance—bringing the rifle out and up from under the topcoat and aiming.

That was as far as he got.

My .45 slug hit him at the bridge of his nose and split his skull like an ax and he toppled onto his side with blood and brains leaking out like he'd done a Humpty Dumpty off the nearby wall. And all the king's horses couldn't do a goddamn thing for this bastard. King's men, either.

People were yelling now, and I heard a police whistle as I approached the corpse.

Something told me conversation with this guy was out.

CHAPTER FIVE

I got to the office at eight the next morning and found Velda already there, with the coffee going and some Danish waiting. She was in a pale yellow silk blouse and a brown skirt whose above-the-knee length was her only concession to changing fashions. She didn't work in heels—she was damn near as tall as me without them.

I'd never made it to my meeting with Hy Gardner and Velda at the Blue Ribbon yesterday afternoon, and had to phone there to call it off from the lobby of Gwen Foster's apartment building. The doorman had let me use the lobby restroom as well, to wash the cabbie's blood off my face.

Wordlessly Velda and I got ourselves cups of coffee and paper napkins for our pastry and went to her desk, where she got behind and sat, and I sat opposite, like a client.

"You've seen the papers," she said.

"Yup."

"They're onto you."

"Yup."

She picked up the *News* from her blotter. "'PRIVATE EYE

IS PUBLIC TARGET.' 'Who's out to get the infamous Mike Hammer?'"

I was half-way through my Danish. "What's the difference between 'infamous' and 'famous,' anyway?"

"You are." She folded the tabloid in half and dumped it with a thunk into the wastebasket by her desk. "And that's the *friendly* paper. The rest dredged up your every kill and self-defense plea going back to the Jack Williams case."

"What can we do about it?" I sipped coffee. I may be tough but I take it with milk and sugar. "Anyway, it might drum up business."

Her eyelids were at half-mast. "Sure. Who doesn't want to do business with a guy with a bull's-eye on his back?"

I shrugged. "Borensen didn't take us off that bridal shower. Did I tell you on the phone last night about both him and Gwen coming over to the park, after they heard what was going on?"

"No, you left that out."

"Well, they did, and backed up my story that I'd had a business meeting with them before taking my innocent leave."

She almost choked on her coffee. She takes it black. "I hope you didn't use the word 'innocent' when Pat showed up. He'd laugh your tail into jail."

"Very poetic, but I told you already. Captain Chambers was fine at the scene. He's concerned about his old pal. Even called me at home last night, after you and I talked."

"Oh?"

I nodded. "It was going on midnight. He'd had a busy evening. Him and maybe twenty other plainclothes cops—looking for witnesses in the park, and talking to tenants in that fancy apartment house with its expensive view on the park."

"What did they get?"

"Bupkus."

"Any evidence in the park?"

"Just the son of a bitch I shot, his rifle and a couple spent shells, one of them mine. I was in the clear from the starting gun."

"Which you fired, of course." The phone on Velda's desk rang and she answered: "Michael Hammer Investigations... Yeah, he just got here." She covered the receiver and said, "Pat. His ears must've been burning."

I got up, tossing my empty coffee cup and wadded napkin down the funnel the *News* made in her wastebasket. "I'll take it in there."

She nodded as I headed into my inner sanctum. I left the door open, though—no secrets between Velda and me. No office secrets, anyway.

"Morning, Pat," I said into the phone, getting behind my desk. "Anything on our dead shooter?"

"That's why I'm calling," his voice said. "Charles Maxwell, thirty-eight, unmarried, former military, and until about three months ago he had a little insurance agency in Baltimore. Sound familiar?"

"It does if the Baltimore PD suspects his agency was a front for a professional killer, though he'd never been charged. Seems to me I've heard that song before."

"Yeah, I thought it was real damn familiar tune, too. I'm having a screwy thought, Mike, and I'm guessing you're having it, too."

"Like someone local recruited Woodcock and Maxwell, bringing them in from cities where their cover was all but blown, offering a fresh start in the same field? And I don't mean insurance."

Pat's sigh spoke volumes. "Yeah. And the question is, how many more imported Woodcocks and Maxwells are out there? Maybe this is a syndicate of hired guns, a new Murder Incorporated, and these relocated hitmen weren't tapped to kill you... their *boss* got the contract."

I grunted a laugh. "I was just an assignment that both assholes blew."

"Elegantly put. Mike, why don't you be reasonable for a change, and keep a low profile until my office can clear this thing up."

"Maybe leave town, you think? Or you could provide me with police protection?"

"Right!"

I hung up on him.

Velda made her liquid way into my office, her pretty mouth twitching with amusement. "You just hung up on the Captain of Homicide."

"Yeah, I'm out of control."

She sat opposite me, no amusement on her face now. "That cabbie's name, according to the papers, was Ernie Jackson. He has a wife and three kids in Harlem. A deacon of his church. A man who welcomed fares into his cab like old friends."

My fists balled of their own volition. "I know. Somebody's going to die for that."

"That's swell, but his family has to live." Her face was smooth, no wrinkles at all, and yet she was frowning at me. "Ernie Jackson got it because he was unlucky enough to have you as a potential passenger."

I frowned back at her, but with every wrinkle my face had to offer. "Think I don't know that? Send them five grand out of our off-the-books stash."

Now the smooth face was somehow smiling. "You want to write a note to go with it? Or I can."

I shook my head. "No. Anonymous. And flowers to the funeral parlor. Nice and big, like he was a horse that won a race. *That* you can sign."

She nodded. "By the way, you look like something the cat dragged in. All those nicks on your face."

"Gives me character."

"I was thinking maybe we should dump the Borensen bridal shower, even if they aren't smart enough to cancel us themselves. We know people who could handle that, and even get a referral fee of our own. I mean, how can you manage it? Your best suit got ruined."

"Good idea." I reached for the phone.

She was really smiling now and rose to go out when she heard me talking with my tailor at Brooks Brothers, telling him I needed another suit with the same specs as last time, and a rush job. Not all Brooks Brothers jobs are cut to conceal a .45 in a shoulder sling.

And when she went out, she wasn't smiling at all.

The next afternoon, at a quarter till three, I was crossing the mosaic-tiled floor of the mile-long lobby of the Waldorf-Astoria, on my way to the tower elevators and the twenty-seventh of the hotel's forty-seven floors. The place had more marble, stone and bronze than Green-Wood Cemetery, and enough eighteenth-century paintings to stock a decent-size museum. And if the Early American furnishings clashed with the Art Moderne touches, nobody seemed to mind. I was skirting over-stuffed chairs and potted plants, making for the bank of elevators, when a bland stocky guy, hatless in a business suit as nice as my new Brooks Brothers, approached and gave a slight head bob. Without a word, we moved in that direction to a nearby couch and sat.

In those pricey threads, Merle Allison might have been a refugee from an executive suite, but he wasn't. He was the chief house dick at the Waldorf with a staff of twenty-five, all of whom dressed as well as their well-off guests, the better to blend in.

Merle had the round, deceptively pleasant face of a top sergeant. He folded his arms and gave me a sideways look. "How dangerous are you making it for my guests, Mike, hanging around my hotel?"

"Congratulations on buying the joint, Merle, and I hope they gave you an employee discount. I don't think anybody's going to take a potshot at me in this lobby, but thanks for your concern."

His smile was warm, his eyes cold. "Well, you never know. If some unknown miscreant is tracking you, there's only so much we can do about it. We have a good security team here, but this facility is open to the public. We're able to discourage dangerous-looking characters and outright riff-raff, but it's an imperfect science. For example, nobody tried to stop you when you came in, did they?"

"No."

"And *you're* armed."

"Does it show?"

"Not particularly. But I'm a detective."

"I heard that rumor. You seem touchy today, Merle."

He lifted an upright finger. "It's this bridal shower on the twenty-seventh floor at four p.m. You're handling security, I understand."

"That's right. Could be that's why I'm armed."

Teeth blossomed in the smile but his eyes remained ice. "You're always armed, Mike. I just don't understand why Mr. Borensen and his fiancée needed to bring you in. We offered to provide security ourselves. Aren't we good enough?"

"You know, Merle, when I got the call, I probably should have said, 'Never mind paying me a grand and a half, Mr. Borensen. You'll do just fine with hotel security.'"

His face fell, and the smile went with it. "You're getting fifteen hundred for a couple of hours work? That's highway robbery."

"It's the indoor variety Borensen is concerned about."

I explained my client's thinking, but also admitted that I was a kind of celebrity attraction. Part of the entertainment.

Allison had cooled down. "Well, you always were more entertaining than me, Mike. I guess I don't begrudge you turning a dollar. Even fifteen hundred of 'em."

"Big of you." I put on a friendly face. "Listen, buddy, I could use a favor."

"Yeah?"

"This affair today is being catered by the hotel. Will there be any help brought in, or will it be strictly staff?"

"Staff."

"You know them all?"

"Enough to recognize. This hotel has more employees than

guest capacity, you know." He shrugged in false modesty. "But I stay on top of hirings and firings."

"Good. I'm going up to brief them right now. Would you tag along, and make sure there are no unfamiliar faces?"

Merle agreed to that, and as we went up in the west tower elevator, he asked me how I'd managed to get shot at twice in one week. He didn't mean to pry.

"It'd be prying," I said, "if you asked how it felt to kill two guys in one week."

"How *does* it feel, Mike?"

"A hell of a lot better than being dead."

In the suite, we moved across a light-green marble floor through an entryway bordered by Grecian busts on white pillars, a faux antiquity touch at odds with the otherwise modern furnishings.

By the side wall to my right, two facing coral-leather couches were perpendicular to a white marble fireplace over which hung a big room-doubling mirror. A low-slung glass-topped table perched between the couches, all positioned on a white throw rug as fluffy as egg whites on their way to being meringue. At the far end of this high-ceilinged living room, a triptych of windows presented a panoramic Manhattan skyline. Nearby, on the right wall, a door would lead to a bedroom, assuming this was set up like similar Waldorf suites I'd been in.

But all of this was somewhat lost in the flowers, so many flowers, roses, lilies, tulips, some yellow, some white—the bride-to-be's colors—on tabletops, on the mantel, elaborate arrangements on virtually every surface except cushions designed for backsides.

Velda was already there. She'd wanted to be on hand as the

help arrived. Right now she was in the dining room, where—off to the left, filling much of the space—chairs were arranged in groups of four or five at small linen-covered tables, enough to accommodate the fifty guests who'd soon be arriving. The tables and chairs faced a white baby grand in front of another Cinerama window onto the city. I viewed all this from just inside the open French doors.

The dining room table, draped in linen and arrayed with presents, had been moved closer to the facing wall. A fair number of gifts bore the light blue, white-ribboned boxes that whisper-screamed Tiffany's. The rest were mostly wrapped in yellow and white, to go with the floral arrangements much in evidence here, as well.

Velda, in a black cocktail dress with bare sleeves and a rather full short skirt, had positioned herself near the gift table. Meanwhile, scattered on chairs at the little tables, primed by Velda, the party's staff sat waiting to get a pep talk from me. On the young side, mostly in their twenties and early thirties, they seemed to be college kids needing a part-time job or former college kids who needed a job period.

I counted ten of them—five male, five female, attractive, slender, all in black trousers, ruffled white shirts and bow ties— and two more, a woman and a man, unattractive, heavy-set, in cook's whites. The latter pair worked the little kitchen, prepping platters of hors d'oeuvres and trays of martinis.

A few of these staffers nodded to Merle, seeing him at my side. The well-dressed house dick scanned the room slowly, gave me a nod that they were all legit, and took his leave.

I gave them their special instructions. I explained that I would be in the living room where I could keep an eye on the door while Velda would watch the gift table.

One young man had already been assigned to greeter duty, which included taking coats and depositing them on the bed in the bedroom, as if this high-society bridal shower were a suburban house party.

"As far as any attendee is to know," I told them, "Miss Sterling is just another guest, an out-of-town friend of Miss Foster's."

A kid in back raised a hand as if in class.

"Yeah?" I said.

"Mr. Hammer, is there anything we should be doing differently? How seriously do you take the threat of a robbery?"

"Unless you see something really suspicious, just do your job. Miss Sterling and I will take care of the rest."

"What would you consider 'really suspicious?'"

"A guest, after the gifts are opened, slipping something into a purse. One of you trusted hotel employees turning out to have pickpocket skills, helping yourself to a nice diamond bracelet, would be another."

Some of them smiled at that, others looked alarmed.

"Anything like that you might see," I said, "report to me."

Nods all around.

"And while it's not likely," I said, "if armed robbers should burst in here—and Miss Sterling and I don't nip it in the bud— just do as they ask. And encourage our guests to do the same."

A young woman, her voice quavering, asked, "Mr. Hammer, we aren't in danger of being in the middle of... of some kind of... *shoot-out*, are we?"

"We won't endanger anyone," I said.

"That's a promise," Velda said.

No one had any further questions.

With the conclusion of my spiel, they rose from their chairs at the guest tables and lined up at the back of the room, a little army ready for further orders. It was three-thirty now.

A few minutes later, Gwen Foster showed up on the arm of Leif Borensen. She was in a bright yellow cocktail dress with a simple strand of pearls, very chic, but looking too young for her own party. Borensen was in a light yellow sweater and tan slacks, expensively casual. He looked too old for the party. Also the wrong sex.

As they came in—Gwen had a key—Borensen grinned at me and held up his hands in surrender.

"I know I'm not supposed to be here," the big Viking said, "but I just wanted a quick look at the place… So many flowers, honey!"

She was holding his hand tight, her big blue eyes wide, dominating her delicate, pretty features. "I know! So wonderful. Doesn't it smell like a garden? I hope none of my girl friends has hay fever."

They took a quick tour, still hand-in-hand, and stopped to take in the table of gifts.

"What a *haul* you're making, honey!" he said to her.

Velda had slipped up at my side. "She really is," she whispered to me.

"Yeah, I saw the Tiffany boxes."

"The rest won't be too shabby, either. Know where her bridal registry was? Saks."

Borensen ducked out, and soon the guests started arriving. The guy working the door looked out his peep hole, then collected coats, and I nodded to the members of the high-class chorus line that gradually came in. Like the wait staff, they were in their twenties and early thirties, beauties who seemed to be walking right out of the society pages.

Not that every doll was of the wealthy class—some were showbiz friends of Gwen's, *real* chorus-line members. And it was a snap to tell which category a girl belonged to because Gwen greeted every one of them, making each feel special, and all I had to do was pay attention to the chatter. I did that in part because if any one of this pulchritudinous parade was a sneak thief, it'd most likely be one of the struggling actresses or chorines.

On the other hand, a lot of rich people are nuts, so it wasn't out of the question a former debutante might be suffering so much in her wealth-riddled despair that she'd turned klepto.

As the guests formed pairs or little groups, there was some pointing and giggling at me, school girls discussing the new kid. Of course I was anything but a new kid. More like an old teacher. But my media fame/infamy made me a topic of conversation. For fifteen hundred bucks, I did not give a shit.

Before long the shower was in full sway, the young women in cocktail dresses, bright colors mostly and nicely short, spread out over both rooms, having a wonderful time chatting and sipping martinis. The waiters and waitresses threading through didn't get many takers on the hors d'oeuvres—this was a group watching its collective figure.

And, brother, I was watching them, too.

A stereo was playing the latest rock 'n' roll, which seemed slightly incongruous to me, but at least it was soft. Maybe a third of the girls were smoking but the ventilation was good, and anyway cigarettes were props to them, rarely puffed.

Velda drifted in to check up on me. She saw me standing there with a silly grin on my face and got a smirk going.

"They sure hired a fox to guard the chicken house," she said.

"Some pretty foxy chickens, if you ask me."

"I didn't ask you."

I pointed. "You need to get back to your post, soldier."

"That rates an elbow, but the trouble is… you're right, Mike. Have you *seen* the rocks on display?"

I had. The cocktail dresses were simple, not a patterned print in the place, strictly solid colors, all very pop art. Maybe half the wenches wore hats, all at least as crazy as the puffy red number Gwen sported the other day. But the jewelry on necks and wrists was very old-fashioned—diamonds and emeralds and rubies, oh my.

"I can see why Borensen wanted armed security," I said to Velda. "His two-hundred grand estimate might be low."

She nodded toward that bedroom door in the corner of the fireplace wall. "There's a way in through the bedroom, you know."

"Yeah. I scoped that out. Probably too much activity for anybody to risk it."

"All it would take is a passkey or an accomplice. Do it when the living room is full and you could just slip in."

"If you were a female in a cocktail dress, maybe."

"Or a young male or female in black slacks, white shirt and bow tie."

She wasn't wrong. But I said, "It's still risky. That's where the facilities are."

"Well, you're right about that. Even the rich and famous have to tinkle and poo."

"You are such a classy broad."

That made her laugh, and she went back to assume her post. Watching her go, with those long, mostly exposed legs, made all these other dolls look like also-rans.

For about an hour, the cocktail-party vibe held sway, but then the girls assembled in the dining room for the entertainment. Bobby Short, a young colored cabaret singer and pianist making a name for himself, had arrived around four-thirty, and had done some mingling. But now, with that stereo silenced, it was time for him to do his thing, which was jazzy takes on Rodgers and Hart and Cole Porter and other real songwriters.

The living room emptied out for his performance, and I was left alone to watch the door. But it was unlikely anybody invited would show up this late. Even the young man taking coats had bailed for martini duty. At least I could hear the smoky-voiced song stylings from the other room.

Around six o'clock, I let the cabaret singer out, while in the other room the jewel-clad cuties were watching Gwen open presents, with Velda handing each one to her, the hostess thanking each gift giver to applause while Velda wrote down the name of the gift and the giver in a book.

That left me alone in the living room with only the occasional babe cutting through to use the bedroom john. Most of them flicked me a smile that said they were a little embarrassed I'd discovered they were human.

The detective stuff people read about is exciting, even thrilling. But what we mostly actually do is dishwater dull. This had been boring duty, nicely mitigated by all the female goodies on show. I strolled to the open French doors where I had a view on Gwen and Velda doing the presents routine.

Man, all that swag was something—if there were any fondue sets or blenders in there, they must be sterling silver, because it seemed like everything else was. The girls at their tables were laughing and clapping and doing more ooohing and aaahing, getting loud about it—frankly they were all probably at least a little tipsy. That's probably why I didn't hear him.

But I heard Velda, all right, and saw her wide-eyed alarm as she said, "*Mike! Down!*"

I didn't argue, and as I hit the deck, I caught Velda whipping her little automatic out from the thigh holster under that full skirt and three shots were flying over my head, cracks that *one-two-three* turned the hen party into a screaming, all-out zoo.

I looked back fast enough, still on my belly, to see a bland-faced guy in a white shirt, bow tie and black trousers take all three of Velda's shots in his chest, with immediate blossoms of red soaking the white, not going with the bride's colors at all. He slid down the bedroom door, leaving smeary snail trails of scarlet and sat there with his chin on his chest and dead eyes staring at nothing, the nine-millimeter automatic clunking to the floor from lifeless fingers.

The girls weren't screaming now, but they were talking, loud and upset, those who weren't shocked into a stunned silence, anyway.

Velda was at my side, helping me up. "You all right, Mike?"

"Just wounded pride," I said, on my feet. "And you know what? I'm starting to feel unpopular."

CHAPTER SIX

I called headquarters from the suite's bedroom and Pat said he'd be over with a team straightaway. Then I phoned down to Merle Allison's office. The line was busy and I had to try the front desk to have them send somebody over to the security office and tell Merle there had been a shooting in Suite 2757.

When the well-dressed stocky house dick arrived, not quite five minutes later, he told me he'd missed my call because he was on the phone dealing with guests on the twenty-seventh floor asking about gunshots.

"Velda has rounded up the guests and the hostess in the dining room," I said. "The wait staff and the two cooks, too. Would you keep an eye on them till Captain Chambers gets here?"

Merle was feeling territorial again. "Who put you in charge, Hammer?"

"The guy who came here to shoot me."

"I thought it was a heist."

Maybe Merle *was* a detective—he'd put his finger on the crux of it, hadn't he?

"Would you rather stand guard over a corpse," I asked him,

"or ride herd on a bunch of young lookers?"

The round face thought about that for about half a second, then spelled Velda in the dining room.

She joined me where I was kneeling over the dead fake waiter.

"He's in his thirties, I'd say," she said, crouching down in her cocktail dress, its full skirt making that easy. "Very average-looking. I don't suppose he's got a wallet on him."

"I checked. No, and of course that's no surprise. The gun is a Browning nine millimeter. What do you make of that?"

I pointed to a square of folded white cloth stuffed in his waistband, like a big hanky.

"Laundry bag," she said. "For the take."

I got to my feet. She did the same. We went over and took one of the coral couches in front of the marble fireplace. The murmur of the girls in the next room was like an engine purring.

I said, "He figured to stuff all that sterling silver from the other room in a *laundry* bag?"

"Maybe he was just after the jewels."

I grinned at her. "Is that what you really think, doll?"

Her smile was more subtle. "Of course not. He was here to kill you. The robbery is just a cover. He may have gone ahead and carried it out... but taking you down was the idea."

I tossed an upraised palm. "But why bother? Did Woodcock bother with a cover when he invaded our office? Did the guy who killed that poor cabbie do anything but start blasting in broad daylight from a city park?"

She was slowly shaking her head. "Doesn't make a bit of sense to me, Mike."

But I was thinking. "It might to me, only it'll take some digging."

"Well, that's what we do."

"Right. Let me handle Pat."

She clutched my sleeve. "Mike… you didn't kill that intruder. *I* did."

I patted her hand. "I know. So give him a brief statement and then say you're way too upset over killing a guy to do any more talking."

The brown eyes narrowed. "And Pat will buy that?"

"Sure. You're his weakness. You *are* okay?"

A smirk. "What do you think?"

Pat arrived with a small army of plainclothes men and lab guys including a photographer. He never took off his fedora and trenchcoat the whole time he was there, maybe to remind everybody he was a cop. I gave him a quick rundown, and, skirting the corpse, showed him the hall door in the bedroom that the guy had come in. The bed was still piled with the coats of the female attendees, lots of dead minks trying to mate.

Back in the living room, I kept my distance as he sat with Velda on the coral couch and got a preliminary statement out of her.

Then she said, "Is that enough for now? I'm really beside myself about this."

Pat's gray-blue eyes studied her like a forensics exhibit. Then, finally, he said, "Did Mike tell you to say that?"

"What do you mean?"

"I mean, Velda—you've killed guys before."

"Not as many as Mike."

"Who has?"

But he just waved a hand, dismissing her, and she found a chair in a quiet corner of the living room, where she pretended to be freaked out while she kept an eye on what the team of technicians were up to, and what they were finding.

Now I sat with Pat, only I took one couch and he took the other, facing each other over the low-slung coffee table.

"So what do you make of this, Mike?"

"Looks like a robbery. My client was afraid somebody might try something. That's why Velda and I were here, you know."

He gave me half a smile. "I don't want to tax your memory, chum, but this is the third time this week somebody tried to kill you."

"This prick didn't try to kill me. He came in that door with a gun in his hand, with all that swag in mind, and I just happened to be in the room he entered into. *I* didn't shoot him, remember."

"Velda shot him." He sucked in breath. "It stinks."

"Why, what do *you* think this is?"

"It's the third damn time somebody's targeted you. And this is getting out of hand. What I should do is take you into protective custody."

"Why? I'm not a witness."

His eyes blazed. "The hell you aren't! You were right here when the guy came in!"

"But he's dead." I kept it low-key. Nice and innocent. "Do you suspect an accomplice among those girls in the next room?"

He was frowning. "It's possible, isn't it? And there's wait staff. How many?"

"Ten. Five of each sex, and two cooks."

"And if any one of them went off to use the john, she or he could have let that bogus waiter in through the bedroom door."

"Possible. As I see it, you've got sixty-two people to question, plus various staff members here at the Waldorf. You should probably get started."

He frowned. "My boys are already on that."

"Sure, and they'll take names and numbers and addresses, and that's all, for now. You'll look into them individually and that'll take weeks. Like I said, maybe you should get started."

Pat sighed. His hands were on his knees. "Mike—who's trying to kill you?"

"I don't know, Pat. Really don't. I haven't even looked into it yet. I mean, you said you were investigating. I've just been waiting by the phone for you to call."

"Screw you, buddy." He threw up his hands. "You've got *Velda* caught up in this now! Do the right thing. Cooperate."

My palms patted the air. "Okay, okay. Let's, for the sake of argument, say you're right. This is a robbery that was a sham, and it was really all about me. But why bother with this elaborate set-up? The first two attempts made no such pretense."

"Maybe not the second, outside of Borensen's apartment house. But the first one, the guy might have intended to stage a burglary after he took you down. Hell, that's how the newspapers handled it."

"Because your public affairs office handed out a bullshit story. Be fun to see how those flacks handle this one."

From behind Pat, one of the techs called out: "*Captain!* Come take a look."

He got up and went over. I lighted up a Lucky and put my feet on the coffee table. I blew smoke rings. He wasn't gone long.

Settling back down, he said, "Probably no accomplice. He had a hotel passkey in his pocket."

"So the girls are in the clear."

He nodded. "But maybe not the wait staff. They're hotel employees, after all. And that passkey came from somewhere on site."

"Right. They got about fifteen hundred employees here. You should talk to all of them. Better get going."

He suddenly looked very tired.

"Mike," he said, "I'm just trying to keep you alive."

"I appreciate that, buddy. I really do. But that's my job."

He shook his head, slowly. "No, actually, it's mine. And I want to know why anybody would go to the trouble of setting up a fake robbery so you could be a casualty. Any thoughts on that subject?"

"Not yet."

"That sounds like you *do* have something cooking in that skull of yours."

"Cooking. Not done. Not ready for consumption."

He accepted that—not that he had much choice.

I said, "Not to tell you your business, but you should start by talking to the hostess—my client's bride-to-be, Gwen Foster. I'll introduce you, if you like."

He nodded again, too distracted and tied up in mental knots to realize I was just trying to horn in on the interview. He got up and I put out the smoke and walked with him into the dining room where all the guests and staffers remained corralled, the former at their tables, the latter along the back wall, like a line-up at headquarters.

I introduced Pat to Gwen and said he was a good guy and

that she should be frank with him. (Since *I* wasn't going to be, somebody ought to.) I suggested the little kitchen and Pat thought that was a good idea.

We sat at a table for four. The tabletop was clear, all of the trays and food preparation items either on the counters or the stove. A coffee urn allowed me to provide cups for all three of us. And there was milk and sugar for me.

Pat asked Gwen who knew about today's bridal shower besides the invited guests. She didn't really know offhand, but did say she'd made no secret of it. He requested a list of anybody who'd been invited but declined or just didn't show, and she said she could put that together.

She always looked young to me, but right now she was like a wounded baby bird. A wounded baby bird in a bright yellow dress. Her blonde hair was askew and the big blue eyes were dazed. But she did all right with the questions.

"From where I stood," she said, looking into nothing, not unlike the way the dead intruder had stared at the floor, "I saw everything. I saw the man come in with a gun, I saw him aim it toward Mr. Hammer's back, I saw Miss Sterling react and heard her shout a warning and Mr. Hammer went down fast, and then... I saw the rest, too. Terrible. Horrible."

I thought she might cry, so I had a napkin ready for her to do that into. Which she did.

But Pat was looking at me. "Miss Foster says the guy was pointing his gun at you. At your back. Velda just said he had a gun in his hand."

I shrugged. "He was pointing it toward those open French

doors, where all the people and the loot was. I was just between him and it. Not unnatural for an armed robber to realize a security guy is in the way, and do something about it."

Somebody came in and it was Borensen, still in the sweater and slacks. Worry had lengthened his face into a woeful mask.

He went to where Gwen sat and stood there with a hand on her shoulder. "Darling, are you…?"

She flew to her feet and into his arms. He comforted her and I gave Pat a look and we both went out, giving them some privacy.

"That's your client," Pat said. "Borensen."

"That's my client. Borensen."

"How about him?"

"How about him."

"I mean… does he have a reason to want you dead?"

"I just met him, Pat. He's been living in California for twenty years."

"But he used to be in New York. Maybe you had a run-in back then, something that's slipped your mind—maybe back in your drinking days, and—"

"Pat, I said I just *met* him. And he didn't even come to me first—he went to the Smith-Torrence boys. This is a damn referral! Anyway, why the hell would he disrupt his fiancée's bridal shower to stage a fake robbery and a real killing?"

"I don't know. I was hoping maybe you would."

Borensen came out of the kitchen, alone. He worked up a brave smile. "She's doing all right. She's doing better. You're Captain Chambers?"

"That's right."

"I'm sure you have some questions."

Pat nodded and walked him out through the dining room where his plainclothes guys were going from table to table, writing down information, taking their time. Some of these guys would never get closer to a beautiful woman.

I followed the homicide captain and my client into the living room, where Pat turned to me, with a mild frown. Over by the door, lab boys were still working on the dead guy, who was currently posing for pictures.

"Mike, do you mind?" Pat said. "I'll just have a private word or two with Mr. Borensen."

"Sure."

I found my way to Velda's quiet corner. I knelt by her chair. "Anything interesting?"

"That was a laundry bag in his waistband, all right. Also, he had a spare nine mil magazine in his vest pocket."

"Was he expecting a gun fight?"

"If he was taking on Mike Hammer, would that be so crazy?"

She had me there.

When Pat was done with him, Borensen came over to me, shaking his head glumly.

"Nobody is more shocked than I am, Mr. Hammer, that I was right about this. That there was a genuine possibility of a robbery attempt."

I shrugged. "With over two hundred grand in jewels and gifts on dock, you were right to hire security. You'd have been negligent not to. And in a public place, like a hotel, well...."

His handsome features clenched with concern. "Could this

have anything to do with the attempts on your life? Could this be another such attempt, and not *really* a robbery try at all?"

"It's possible, Mr. Borensen. And I'm going to find out. And if that's what this is—an attempt on my life, using the bridal shower as a cover—I will promise you one thing."

"Yes?"

"You're getting a refund."

After a quiet dinner at a neighborhood Italian joint, Velda and I wound up on her couch in front of a crackling fire. The evening was just cold enough to provide an excuse. I was in slacks and my undershirt and she was in a blue terry-cloth robe, cuddled up to me.

Though Velda and I were not living together, our apartments were in the same building—strictly for business convenience, of course, if you're naive enough to buy that.

"Kitten," I said, "you *are* all right, right?"

"I'm fine."

"Not everybody has my mental make-up."

"Really?"

"I mean, if killing some bastard bothers you, I understand."

"Who says you aren't a sensitive man?"

"Honey, I just mean…"

"I know what you mean."

She looked lovely in the cradle of my arm, washed with lightly flickering orange and blue from the fireplace glow, eyes shut, but only half-asleep. Maybe she really was bothered, troubled by today's violence. That was only human. Or so I've been told.

She hugged me and buried her face in my chest and when my T-shirt got wet, I realized she was quietly crying.

"Cry your eyes out, baby," I said. "Make it go away. Just know that guy is no great loss to mankind, just another asshole with a rod who needed killing."

She started laughing, but she was still crying, too. She looked up at me with a wide smile and her eyes pearled with tears. "You big dumb lug of an Irish son of a bitch."

I smiled back at her. "Is that what I am?"

"I'm not crying for that creep. I'm crying because… I don't want to *lose* you. And everybody in this town but me and Pat wants you dead."

"I'm not sure about Pat."

That made her laugh, and then we were hugging, and what happened next on that couch is nobody's business but ours.

Around ten I was climbing in bed in my shorts when the phone rang on Velda's nightstand. She frowned over at me. Ten was a little late for anybody to be calling.

"Answer it," I said.

She did, sitting up; she was in a black sheer thing that could still get her in trouble, no matter what had happened on that couch. My recuperative powers were surprising for a man my age.

"Yes?… Hello, Pat. Uh, yes, he is here. We were just having a late dinner." She looked at me wide-eyed and shrugged, as if to say, *Is he dumb enough to buy that?*

She and I swapped sides of the bed and I took the call.

I said, "Don't tell me you're still working, chum."

"I am. You keep me busy."

"I'm guessing you wouldn't be tracking me down if you didn't have something."

"I have something, all right. Like a rundown on today's would-be shooter? I mean, we better keep up with this or we might fall behind."

"How did you get something on him so fast?"

"He had car keys on him, and we located the car in the Waldorf's parking garage. His name on the license led us to his apartment and we found material that indicates he was, until four months ago, a resident of Detroit. His ex-wife's contact material was on hand, and we called her. She was not sad to learn of her ex's demise, since he was an alimony cheat. She told us the police had been interested in him, and to make a long story shorter, I called a friend on the Detroit PD who told us a very familiar tale."

"Not another insurance agent."

"Travel agent. Robert Hastings, thirty-six. Suspected in several homicides thought to be killings for hire. Ex-military, no strings except the ex, no kids."

"Okay, so it wasn't a robbery."

"You never thought it was."

"No, I didn't. But if people think that's what it was, it'll make investigating these kill attempts easier."

"Don't be a chump, Mike. This is the third try on you in a week, in case you didn't hear me the other times, and the third hired gun you took down."

"No, Velda took this one down."

"Yes, yes, yes, I know. But the Hammer *team* took him down, okay?"

"Okay. What do you want from me, Pat?"

"Cooperation. Let's work on this together."

He couldn't see me shaking my head, but it was in my voice. "Why don't you pursue your investigation, and I'll pursue mine, and we'll compare notes when something comes up."

"Compare notes, and then when you know, or *think* you know, who's behind all this, you'll kill the guy, just goddamn kill him, and I'll get the self-defense phone call from you. Which is your idea of 'comparing notes.'"

"Considering how many cases I've cleared up for you," I said, "that's not at all gracious."

I hung up on him.

Velda, on her side facing away from me, now looked back with a smile. "You hung up on the Captain of Homicide again."

"I thought he had a bad attitude."

She was giggling when she fell asleep.

Not crying. That was a big improvement.

When the phone rang again, it woke both of us on the first trill, and we were bolt upright as if from a bad dream we'd somehow shared. She looked past me at the nightstand clock near the ringing phone—three-oh-five in the morning. She frowned at me. I shrugged and picked up the phone.

"This better be important, Pat," I said, leaning on an elbow now.

"Oh, it's important," an unfamiliar voice said. A quiet, calm voice, male, medium-pitched, almost soothing, like a late night disc jockey playing the kind of records that helped insomniacs finally drift off.

But I was wide awake, and sitting up.

"Okay, buddy," I said. "You got two choices—hang up and never call this number again, or give me a name and a reason for calling in the middle of the night."

"Technically it's morning," the soothing voice said. "But I hope you won't hang up. It's time we talked. It's really time."

"Who is this?"

"An admirer. Oh, I know Mr. Woodcock was an admirer of your work, too, and I rather suspect that got in the way of him carrying out his assignment properly."

Nothing like that had been in the papers.

I gave Velda a bug-eyed look, and covered the mouthpiece, whispering harshly, "Get the extension."

She slipped out of bed and ran off to get the phone on the kitchenette wall.

"Is that Miss Sterling picking up another line?" he asked. "I'm a big fan of yours, as well, Velda… if I may. And Mike… again, if I *may*… I hope you know how lucky you are to have someone like Velda in your life. That's something I've never had, never enjoyed."

"What do you want?"

"Just to talk to you. I think it's time I let you know what exactly is going on."

"Why don't you?"

"If you heard my name, it would mean nothing. And if I were

to give you a list of those I've killed... *personally* killed... you would quickly put together that none of these homicides were ever connected by law enforcement. They have no idea of my existence. And many of my contracts... because I am the premiere contract killer who ever walked this dark, sad, miserable excuse for a planet... a good number were written off as accidents. But that's not a fitting fate for you. Not for Mike Hammer. You've killed so *many*. In some respects I'm a piker, compared to you. That's the point."

If he'd called the office, I could have hit a switch and recorded the call. But he knew not to call there. Worse, he had Velda's number. Neither of us were listed. Bad. Very bad.

"What *is* the point?" I asked.

"I'm going to be... retiring soon. I have been looking for a challenge, one last... not job, but kill... to feel, to *know*, that I've gone out on top. That no one was in my league, my class. So naturally you've been on my mind, Mike."

"So this is no contract somebody took out on me. Just a lunatic at work."

"No need to insult me, Mike. We're never going to be friends, I realize, but we can certainly be colleagues in our shared pursuit. Friendly adversaries, let's say, each with the proper respect for the other. I'm a killer, Mike, and you're a killer, so we are brothers in blood. Do you understand?"

"I'm starting to."

"As it happens, my decision was made for me by fate. Do you believe in fate, Mike? In destiny?"

"I call it kismet."

"Ah. How poetic. Well, at the very time, very *moment* I was thinking of… let's call it *challenging* you to a kind of game of wits, a duel of giants… I was approached by an individual who wanted you dead. Imagine that! Is this the hand of someone bigger than either of us, moving chess pieces? Are we merely pawns in some grander game than we can comprehend? Be that as it may, when I was hired to kill you, I knew I was meant to determine which of us was the killer among the killers. Like they say at the prize fights, Mike—the cham-*peen*."

"Then why send Woodcock, and these other two clowns? Why the bogus robbery today?"

"I have my ways and I have my reasons."

"What are they?"

"Well… as for the other three instances, I wanted to determine whether you were worthy of my challenge. If a journeyman contract man had no trouble wiping you out, well… you wouldn't be worthy of my attention. So I've dispatched three such men… and you've dispatched *them*. I'm coming to the conclusion that you are indeed worthy."

"Thanks. So let's meet somewhere and see how this plays out. Or is your idea of a 'challenge' to shoot from a rooftop?"

"Are you suggesting there should be *rules* here? Now that's disappointing. The great rule-breaker wants rules! No, it could come at any time, Mike. You should look up, down and around and behind you. Just know that if you look behind you, I'll tag you from the front."

And he clicked off.

CHAPTER SEVEN

At P.J. Moriarty's steak and chop house on Sixth and Fifty-second, Velda and I sat in the bar across from Hy Gardner in a booth we were lucky to have. Mid-evening, the endless line of stools was full and the restaurant beyond was hopping, producing a drone of conversation punctuated by clinking glass and an occasional dropped dish, making for real privacy.

We ate first and talked no business. My kind of business, like what had happened yesterday afternoon in an elegant suite at the Waldorf-Astoria, did not make for polite table talk, even in my circles.

Then we settled in for drinks and the real reason I'd called this meeting. And I didn't even have to call it to order.

"I made a few more inquiries," Hy said, a tumbler of bourbon in one hand, a plump cigar in the other. The way he was peering at me over the glasses said he'd really come up with something.

I'd already filled him in on the phone about the party crasher at the bridal shower, giving him more than the papers had.

The columnist's blue suit and darker blue tie were typically crisp, but his face sagged from a long day. In addition to making long-distance calls for me, he'd been in his suite at the Plaza since breakfast, interviewing Broadway actors and directors about their upcoming productions.

"Your client Leif Borensen has what we call in the newspaper trade 'hidden levels,'" he said. "And I'm not talking about depth of character. More like the show business equivalent of cover stories."

"Like the starlet who was a straight-A schoolgirl from Topeka," I said, "but really a B-girl from Boston. That kind of level?"

He nodded, tamped cigar ash into a PJM glass tray. "Only in this case we're talking about a rich aunt who died but was never alive in the first place."

The rich aunt bit had always seemed too convenient to me.

"If a windfall inheritance didn't fund his real estate schemes," Velda said, leaning forward, "who *did* back Borensen?"

"Before I deal with that," Hy said, exhaling smoke that had been in Havana before it made it to his lungs, "let me ask you both a question. How hard is it to raise money for independent movie productions?"

"Plenty hard," I said. "And a pain in the tail. You have to go around begging nickels and dimes from dentists and doctors or maybe actual rich relatives."

Velda put in, "Or if you already have a track record, you might scrounge up some advance sales from distributors based on a scary, sexy poster for a picture that hasn't rolled film yet."

"There's another way," Hy said, and a smile curled on that glum, anteater mug of his. "We have a group of individuals right here in Manhattan who *often* invest in motion pictures, particularly independent ones."

And I got it right away. "Mob money."

Velda got it, too, and snapped her fingers. "Borensen was a money laundry!"

Hy nodded sagely. "That's the word I get. And he still *is*, as far as I can tell. The handy thing about the movie business, and television syndication as well, is that you can exaggerate the money you lose, or inflate the money you make, according to which way the wind is blowing."

"Ideal set-up," I said.

Hy went on: "And Borensen did a lot of his own distribution, to drive-ins with the flicks, and to local TV stations with his syndicated shows. Even a correspondence school accountant would find cooking those kind of books about as tricky as boiling water."

I asked, "How did a smalltime New York actor get in bed with the lasagna lads in the first place?"

Hy sipped some bourbon before answering. "Well, as we know, back when he was starting out, Borensen was not exactly giving Brando and James Dean much competition. But he worked steady enough, and had access enough, on both stage and small screen... and a lot of TV was in New York back then, remember... to support himself with a profitable sideline."

"Drug dealer," I said.

Hy smiled a little, impressed by my perspicacity. He said, "Like the old ladies down in Florida say, bingo. Grass and pills and, who knows, maybe coke and heroin. My info isn't that specific on that particular, uh, score."

Frowning, Velda asked, "Is this theory or fact?"

"I have it on good authority it's fact," Hy said. "But I had to dig for it *and* call in some markers. This is anything but public knowledge back in L.A. And those in the know usually keep such things to themselves, or at most refer to them vaguely."

"Show business has a long history," I said, "of looking the other way where mob funding is concerned."

Velda smirked. "Just ask the headliners in Vegas."

They were piping in Sinatra right now.

Hy said, "Borensen's move back to New York may mean he's splitting from the boys, and going legit. Or he could be expanding operations for them. Either way you slice it, hooking up with Martin Foster, and now tying the knot with the late Foster's successful actress of a daughter? That's a big, a *very* big, step up for our golden boy in the producing game."

"If I'd been butting heads with the Mulberry Street crowd lately," I said, "I'd think Borensen's been setting me up for them."

Velda said, "Our man Leif was certainly in a position to do that. In these most recent two instances, he knew right where you'd be, Mike—first with the meeting at his apartment house, then with the bridal shower."

Hy was staring me down. "Mike—is there something you're not thinking of? Something involving the mob that might prompt them to use Borensen to tee you up for a hole in one?"

I shrugged. "I don't see what. These days I'm strictly a working P.I., pursuing no grudges and not generating any, either."

Velda said, "There *must* be *something*."

I shrugged again and looked across the booth at my old friend.

"Well…" Hy started. He paused and stared into his thoughts, flicking off further expensive, illegal ash from his cigar. "…it's a little thing, but there might be one item of interest. Of possible pertinence. But I don't see the connection to you, Mike."

"Let me be the judge," I said.

The columnist grunted a laugh. "Why not? You've been the jury often enough."

That made Velda smile.

He sipped a little bourbon. "I know this oldtime PR guy… well, *knew* him, he's dead now… who was working on the story of his life. We went way back, and he used to feed me items, so… Anyway, last year, before the *Trib* closed its doors, he called wanting to have lunch with me. I said great, love to, talk old times and so on. In a way I hated it, though, because I'd have to lie to him about what a fine idea writing a book on his life story was. Either that, or break it to him that he was just another nobody who nobody heard of, who thinks his life mattered. I mean, how do you break it to a guy who fought his way across Europe that Audie Murphy beat him to it? Like people were out there just waiting with bated breath to read the life story of somebody they never heard of."

As Hy paused for another sip of bourbon, Velda asked, "And was that the case with your old friend?"

He shook his head. "Not at all. I couldn't have been wronger. This was a guy who spent forty years in the trenches of the New York show business scene, and he knew where all the bodies were buried, and who put them there. Everything from abortions to homosexuality to… mob ties. I warned him there could be legal repercussions, or *worse*… but he said at his age, he didn't give a damn. Anyway, he was going to back up his memories with some hard research, to make sure the lawyers wouldn't be scared off and a publisher would take it on."

I asked, "Did he know Borensen back when?"

Hy shrugged, made a face, tamped more ash. "That's what makes this a little thin, Mike. I don't know for sure, but he would almost *have* to have known Borensen, and certainly knew *of* him. And with something as damning as drug dealing in his past, and mob money laundering ever since, Borensen would *flip* if he found out Dick was writing a tell-all."

I leaned forward. "*Dick?* That wouldn't be Dick Blazen, would it?"

"Right. Did you know the guy, Mike?"

I put out my Lucky. "No, but a friend of mine did."

Velda asked, "'*Did*'? Past tense?"

"Very damn past," I said to her. "That's the regular customer who got run down in front of Billy Batson's newsstand last month."

I filled in some blanks for him on the incident—all Hy knew was that Blazen had been hit by a car—including Billy getting a good look at the driver but having no success identifying him, despite numerous line-ups at HQ and going through countless mug books.

Hy rested his cigar in the ashtray and leaned on an elbow. He was peering over the glasses again. "Are you thinking Borensen may have hired a contract killer to remove Dick Blazen? A hit-and-run for hire?"

"Why not?"

My phone caller of the night before had made a point of saying many of his contract kills had been passed off as accidents.

I continued, "On the other hand, maybe Borensen pulled that one off himself."

"If so," Velda said, "all we have to do is show Billy a picture of our client."

Hy said, "Easier said than done. One of the things Dick asked me to help him with was finding pics of various lesser-known but key people he was mentioning in his book. He already had art on many of them, but Borensen was on a short list that Dick needed help with. I checked the *Trib* photo morgue and came up a goose egg. I called around to the other papers and nobody else had anything on the guy either."

Velda asked, "Isn't that unusual? Borensen was an actor on stage and television—several decades ago admittedly—but he's a well-known producer today."

"He was a *minor* actor in his early days," Hy said, "and a schlock producer now. Some of his productions have generated good ink, but the werewolves and sweater babes got the press photos, not him."

"Then," I said to Velda, climbing out of the booth, "we'll haul Billy's behind over to Borensen's apartment right now, for a personal appearance from our client."

Velda was at my side in an eye blink.

"Hold up," Hy said. "Did it ever occur to you that this Billy character might have been paid off?"

"No way," Velda said.

"Billy's okay," I said. "He's Captain Marvel in disguise, you know."

That got a head shake and a laugh out of my cynical pal.

"Good luck, you two," Hy said. "Call me at the Plaza if you get anything newsworthy."

I said, "You're sitting this one out?"

His smile was a friendly fold in a well-used face. "I'm a little long in the tooth to be going down bullet alley any more. But I'll do what I can from the sidelines, starting with taking care of the check."

I gave him a grin of thanks and took Velda by the elbow, heading out.

A light misting rain was just enough to all but empty the sidewalks and make the streetlights hazy. Neon smears turned Manhattan into an impressionist painting, taking the hard edges off and blurring the grime into something damn near romantic.

Neither Velda nor I minded the rain. We walked in it often, sometimes when it was coming down good and hard. Mist we just laughed at. Right now we were both in raincoats, having anticipated a damp evening, and we strolled the few blocks over to Lexington arm-in-arm, as something almost cold enough to be snow put tiny tears all over our faces.

But I won't pretend that this was just another walk in the rain for us. I caught Velda keeping an eye peeled for somebody following, either on foot or on wheels, and outside the restaurant, I'd shifted my .45 to my right-hand trenchcoat pocket. And my hand was in that pocket. Call me over-cautious, but when they keep shooting at you, you can get a little gun shy.

Clutching my left arm, Velda asked, "Assuming Borensen didn't hire it done… what does Billy seeing him run down Hy's friend have to do with one Michael Hammer?"

There was just enough moisture to curl the tips of her black hair into something gypsy-like.

"First," I said, "probably nothing. Second, we don't know for sure Borensen's responsible. We're going to find out."

"And if he did do it?"

I grinned into the mist. "Well, that Viking will get something from me and it won't be a refund. A Viking funeral, maybe."

Billy stayed open till nine-thirty and it was almost that. As we neared, he was just a small figure overwhelmed by the corner newsstand's many magazines, particularly the side displays of comic books. Famous faces smiled at us as we approached. They didn't care about the rain either, but then they were protected by the overhang of the stand.

He was arranging and stacking stuff and didn't see us at first. When he heard our wet footsteps, and turned toward us, the wizened little guy in the plaid cap and flannel jacket had a stack of newspapers in his arms. Seeing Velda, Billy grinned and hugged those papers like he did her in his dreams.

"Hiya, Velda," he said, the way a farmer says Aw Shucks. "When you gonna throw this bum over?"

She beamed at him and put something sultry in it. "I would, Billy, but then who would have me?"

He grinned goofily. "I think you know. I think you do."

Then he acknowledged me with a regular smile; he was standing there between us, like a paperback between a couple of big bookends. He lowered those papers to fig leaf level.

"Y'know, Mike, that pic the *News* ran of you, after that cabbie took your bullet? *Much* better."

I nodded toward Velda. "I took your criticism to heart, Billy. My faithful secretary here sent around a newer shot to all the papers, professionally done—not snapshots from paparazzi rats."

"That kind of off-the-cuff stuff sells a lot of papers, Mike. You got a good business goin'. Don't begrudge me mine."

Right now, this late, there was no business. Lately the city had a habit of emptying out everywhere except the theater district, even before dark. Traffic on the rain-slicked street seemed steady but light.

"Listen," I said, a hand on his shoulder, "I have a lead on that hit-and-runner of yours. How would you like to put his ass away for a long damn time?"

His whole face smiled. "Nothing better. What's the deal, Mike?"

"I may have him identified."

"You got a picture?"

"No, that's the thing. The guy is a ghost where the papers are concerned. Hy Gardner tried every photo morgue in town looking for a pic."

"Hy Gardner," he sighed. The little man shook his head and his half-a-smile was bittersweet. "Them was the days."

"Weren't they just?" I patted his shoulder. "So now if this is the guy, Billy, you're gonna have to put the finger on him. Look right at him, and not in a line-up, either, and say yay or nay. You up to that?"

He was grinning big. "If you're at my side, Mike, I ain't afraid."

I glanced around. What few cars were going by kept right at the limit, taking advantage of the lack of competition, their headlight beams grainy with mist, chasing the pools of light they cast on the reflective surface. If it got any colder, they might get an icy surprise. Meanwhile, the sidewalks remained nearly empty but for the three of us in front of Billy's comic-book-lined stand.

"You mind shutting down to do this, Billy?"

He frowned. It was against his principles to close up early.

I said, "You can't do business in this rain, anyway, Billy my boy. We'll grab a cab and go over to the guy's place."

His eyes widened. "What, he knows we're comin'?"

"Oh, hell no." I grinned. "It'll be a big surprise. But he'll let me in, don't you worry."

"You got that big .45 on you, man?"

"Always."

"Safety off, one in the chamber?"

"You got it."

"Then like somebody wise once said, 'What me, worry?'"

Velda put a hand on Billy's shoulder and said, "Thanks, Billy. This is very important."

Billy lifted the stack of papers and hugged them again just as the dark blue Lincoln slowed at the light in the nearest northbound lane, right next to us. The driver leaned out the window as if to ask quick directions, and that was when I saw the ski mask, and I was going for the .45 in my raincoat pocket, an act that *damnit* slowed me down some, and Velda was clawing her purse for the .32, but the extended snout of the silenced automatic was already pointing out the window and three coughs, like a kid with asthma, told me I had put Velda and Billy in harm's way, just by standing with them.

I had a complex thought that lasted a fraction of a second, and it was how I was going to die in the next instant, the light switch on my life going off, and my arrogance had done it, my belief that I was smarter and bigger and badder than anybody, but nobody is smarter and bigger and badder than three bullets rocketing their way at you.

Only the bullets didn't hit me.

They hit Billy, thunking into those papers he was holding, missing his arms and chewing up newsprint, dotting an I on a headline, the power of those tiny guided missiles taking the little man down onto the pavement in a pile, armful of papers scattering, as faces on magazines smiled and looked everywhere but at him.

And the Lincoln was gone, jumping the light, flashing a license plate spattered with mud on a vehicle otherwise spotless. Other cars were going through an intersection the shooter was on the other side of, and the .45 in my hand couldn't blow him a kiss without risking collateral damage.

Anyway, I was distracted by Velda, who never got her gun out, doing something I'd only heard her do a few times.

Screaming.

CHAPTER EIGHT

Velda's scream trailed into the night as she quickly pulled herself together and joined me, bending over the fallen little man. I peeled the stack of papers away and three slugs stuck out of Billy's heavy padded jacket like misplaced metallic buttons. Just as the cabbie's skull had caused a sniper's bullet to thump me harmlessly in the chest, the thickness of all that newsprint had slowed this deadly trio way down.

But Billy was unconscious and breathing ragged, hit hard by the rounds even if they had stopped short of his body.

"They didn't penetrate," she said, relieved and a little astounded. Her face was moist with mist. "Is he all right?"

I plucked the slugs out, dropped them in my trenchcoat pocket. "He's alive, but he may have broken bones or internal bleeding. We need to get him help."

"When the police get here," she said, a little confused as she stated the obvious, "they'll call an ambulance."

I looked across my fallen friend at Velda and put a hand on her shoulder. "We're going to call one first."

"*What?*"

"That all-night drugstore on Forty-ninth. Get over there and use the phone and call the ambulance service we use. You know the one. Get a wagon over here right now. We're taking over."

I saw the doubt flicker on her face, but then she just nodded, her gypsy ringlets flicking moisture at me, and rose and went off at a brisk pace.

I called out, "Tell them to take Billy to our favorite private hospital! The one outside Newburgh!"

"Figured that," she called, her back to me, and I watched till she was swallowed by the night and the mist.

I got up and went to the little stool Billy used and took the seat cushion off and rested it under his head. Then I sat on the cushion-less stool and lit up a Lucky and thought about killing some people.

The black-and-green-and-white patrol car streaked up the slick street with its siren playing banshee till it rolled to a stop. Two uniforms, one tall and young, the other medium-size but heavy-set and around my age, rolled out.

I gave them a quick report and said, "I already called for the ambulance."

This seemed to satisfy them, but when the heavy-set cop asked for my identification and I handed over my open wallet, his eyes went big, taking in my P.I. badge and ticket.

"Mike Hammer," he said, the way most people say "goddamnit."

"You may want to inform my friend Captain Chambers directly about this," I said, hoping to head off any unpleasantness.

He had a voice like tearing cardboard. "How the hell many shooting incidents have you been in this week anyway, buddy?"

I shrugged, as I took back the wallet. "Depends on how you're counting. It's technically four, but I only returned fire in two." I blew out smoke but resisted the temptation to do it in his face. "Why don't you call it in to Pat Chambers before this gets disagreeable?"

The younger guy, kneeling over Billy, said, "He's alive and there aren't wounds that I can see."

"Like I said," I said, "that stack of newspapers saved him."

"And he's out like a light, breathing heavy," the young cop continued. "Don't see any spent slugs. Holes in his jacket where maybe they hit."

His older partner noted all that but kept his eyes on me. "You were the target here, Hammer?"

"Ask the shooter. Or better still, turn this over to somebody in plainclothes." This time I did let him have the smoke in the pan, but inconspicuously, like maybe it was an accident. "Call Pat Chambers, for instance. Or did I say that already?"

Finally he trundled over to the patrol car and radioed it in to Chambers.

I told the young cop, "There's a kid who fills in for Billy sometimes called Duck-Duck Jones. He also works as a swamper at a dive called the Clover Bar."

"I know of it. What the heck kind of handle is 'Duck-Duck?'"

"I'm going to go out on a limb and say it's a nickname, particularly since his upper teeth stick out to here. I'd advise getting hold of the kid and having him get over here to lock the stand up and be ready to fill in for Billy, if he's hospitalized for a while."

The young cop was nodding. "Good idea… Jeez."

"Jeez what?"

"Will you look at the dish walking down the street? Pretty girl like that shouldn't be out alone, though."

I looked behind me and Velda was on her way back, closing an already short distance. "This one can take care of herself. She's my secretary. I sent her off to call it in."

"I didn't figure she was a streetwalker," he allowed. "Too classy looking."

"I'll tell her that. She'll be highly complimented."

I left the callow cop to figure that one out and went over to meet Velda far enough away that we could talk freely.

"Okay, Mike," she said, almost whispering. "Ambulance should be here any time. Why did I send for it? I mean, I assume you mean to whisk Billy away and keep him out of Pat's hands. *Why?*"

"Who do you think those bullets were for?"

"Well, you of course."

"Wrong. These pro shooters are generally right on target. If that cabbie the other day hadn't stuck his head between me and that bullet, you'd be at a funeral-home visitation about now. No, honey, the guy in that Lincoln shot exactly who he meant to shoot. He just wasn't counting on Billy having that fat stack of papers to slow the slugs."

Her mouth made a scarlet O. "Billy!... You mean, because he witnessed that..."

"I knew you'd catch up, sugar."

She was frowning at me, not angry, but her mind working fast. "Are you saying *Leif Borensen* hired your murder, *and* Billy's? What's the connection?"

"We are. Think about it."

She didn't have to think long, not with those wheels turning like they were. "My God, Mike—your reputation! Your well-deserved, well-known reputation for getting even. Billy's your friend, *our* friend. If somebody took Billy out, you'd be all over it."

"That's right. Hitting me first, or trying to, was a preemptive attack."

But she was shaking her head, having trouble making some of the pieces fit together. "Mike, why didn't that contract killer shoot you tonight as well as Billy? And why not take me down as well?"

I flipped a hand. "Could be a couple of reasons. Maybe it was just a coincidence I happened to be around when the hit on Billy went down, and the shooter knew only that his target was our friend at the newsstand. Or... it could be something even more sinister."

Her eyebrows took a hike. "More sinister than *that?*"

"Yup. Keep in mind our friend on the phone last night. He's been having bad luck with the hired help, in addition to which he's now deemed me worthy of his personal attention. That may have been him tonight."

"But he could have killed you, Mike!"

"No. This is a game to him. A challenge. He's playing with me, Velda. Cat and mouse, and he thinks I'm the mouse. Only he's got a sewer rat by the tail. He figures he can get to me psychologically. Better men, and women, have tried. I have the same psychology as the .45 in my pocket—set me in motion and I go off."

The ambulance came screaming up. It was similar enough to the city variety that the two cops thought nothing of it when a pair of attendants in white brought a stretcher out and strapped

Billy on and hauled him up and into the back of their vehicle. They'd done enough jobs like this for me, and select others, to know to move fast and give any questions from the cops the most perfunctory answers.

But these cops accepted the ambulance at face value, assuming it was from a nearby hospital. They didn't notice the upstate plates, or the lack of certain designations on the side panels. Just not plainclothes material.

"Velda," I said softly, "go home, pack a bag, and drive up to that hospital right now. Get there ASAP, deal with the docs, and camp out in Billy's room. He may still be on the firing line and will need protection. I'll see you later tonight or in the morning, after I've dealt with Pat."

Her eyebrows went up again. "You've been pushing that friendship to the breaking point."

I nodded. "It may take some fancy footwork to stay out of stir this time. I really *am* a material witness on this one."

She nodded, sucked in damp air, and gave me a kiss on the mouth before heading off to catch a cab.

"Where's she going?" the fat cop asked.

"Home."

"You said *she* witnessed this, too!"

"She did. Why, did you want to talk to her? Oh… well, there's a Yellow. Guess she's on her way. Sorry. My oversight."

"Is that what it is. I wonder if Captain Chambers will see it that way, smart-ass?"

* * *

Another patrol car arrived in about five minutes and gave me a lift over to headquarters. This time I only spent fifteen minutes on the bench outside Pat's office. Not time enough to stretch out for a snooze. That was okay. I didn't feel like sleeping.

When the door opened, he gave me a long-suffering look and a thumb over a shoulder. I followed him in, closing the door behind me, and slid into the visitor's chair opposite his desk. He took his time getting to his swivel chair and all but fell into it.

Pat, a consummate professional whose suits were off the rack but well-selected, looked like an unmade bed. He was in his shirtsleeves and his tie was loose and wrinkled. He needed a shave and his eyes were bloodshot.

He growled, "You're having a hell of a week, Mike."

"Maybe, but I look better than you."

He closed his eyes. He opened his eyes. He said, "That's because you don't have to go around cleaning up after yourself. You just wait for me and the rest of the NYPD to do it for you, and if you make a remark about being a taxpayer, I'll slam your ass in the drunk tank."

"You need to get home and get some rest, buddy. What are you doing here, this close to midnight?" I started to get up. "We can do this tomorrow."

"Sit!"

"I'm not a damn spaniel."

"Sit anyway."

I sat.

"Mike," he said, "I've seen the statement you gave to the officers at the scene. Is there anything you'd care to add to it?"

That statement had been factually accurate. So I said, "No. Other than maybe, for hitmen, these guys don't seem to be able to hit much of anything they aim at."

He ignored that. "Let's say I accept everything in your statement. I may want a more formal one, stenographer and the works, but for now… let's say I accept it."

"Let's say that." I dug a Lucky out of the deck and lit it up. It wasn't my fault that having a cigarette in my lips gave me a smirk.

Pat said, "Why don't you add just one little detail. Why don't you tell me where Velda ran off to, just after the shooting? She was there when it went down, at Batson's side just like you were. Where did you send her, Mike?"

I gestured vaguely. "That all-night Rexall's on Lexington and Forty-ninth."

"To get you some aspirin?"

"No, to call the incident in."

"Our dispatcher has no record of that."

"Velda probably didn't give her name. She was a little flustered. She likes Billy."

"Velda. Flustered." He shook his head. "As it happens, we do have a witness, a pedestrian, who called us from a phone booth to report the shooting, and he did give his name, which wasn't Velda Sterling."

"I'd be surprised if it was."

Pat breathed in and breathed out, like a dragon out of lighter fluid. "Do you think I don't know that she called some ambulance service you use? Do you think I don't know that, for some insane reason, you decided to spirit Billy Batson away?"

"I don't know what you know. What am I, psychic?"

"Skip the psyche. You're just sick."

I grinned and the Lucky bobbled. "Decent comeback for a guy who looks about ten minutes shy of passing out. How about some coffee? We could both use it. I've got a smoke for you, if you want to start again."

He reached for the phone like he was going to throw it at me, but instead ordered up some coffee for us. He even made sure mine got milk and sugar. What a pal.

Then he hung up, folded his hands like he was about to lead us in prayer, and said, "I know you have a private hospital you use, somewhere in town, when you want to keep somebody under wraps. You think I don't, Mike?"

Well, it wasn't in town, but that was more than I thought he knew, all right.

I just said, "Don't you know *what* hospital, Pat? I'd think a detective of your caliber would have learned that by now."

"A detective of your caliber, which is .45, should know he's right on the edge of an obstruction of justice charge. If that sticks, you're out of the P.I. business. You won't be able to get a license to sell hot dogs."

"Why, is my fly open?"

He slammed a fist on his blotter and everything on his desk jumped. "You won't be able to get a hunting license for goddamn ducks!"

We sat and glowered at each other, and I let my smoke exit in his general vicinity. Then an almost attractive policewoman who could use some make-up delivered our coffee. We thanked her. She said you're welcome and left.

"Let's try this again," I said. "This time with me asking a few questions."

He sighed, let some coffee roll down his throat, said, "Why not?"

"Who do you make for the target on that street corner tonight?"

He gave me the *you're nuts* look. "What do you mean? *You* were."

"Something I've always wondered," I said, sitting up. "Do you keep separate files on all your cases? You know, so there's no chance of one case brushing up against another and contaminating it."

Only somebody who knew me as well as Pat would have read the sarcasm in my easy tone. His eyes tightened and he leaned forward.

"Okay," he said. "I'm an idiot."

I gestured with an open hand, as if to say, *No argument.*

"Billy was the target," he said, and bounced a fist off his desk. "It's that hit-and-run he saw! He's the only witness who can identify the driver. Damnit. I'm an ass."

I gestured with the open hand again.

Then he pointed a finger at me, a prosecutor indicating the defendant. "But everybody's going to read this thing as another hit attempt on you. The odds of you being involved in three tries on your life *and* an attempt on someone else's life are infinitesimal… Mike, if I look into this as if Billy is the target, I'll get laughed off the force."

"If you don't do that," I said, "you don't deserve to be on the force."

"Do you have a suspect?"

I nodded. "Borensen."

His eyes widened, but soon he was nodding. "Makes sense. Really makes sense. Hell, he could have set you up for the kill twice!"

So I emptied the bag on his desk, gave him everything from Hy's background on Borensen's youthful drug-dealing activities through his mob money laundering past and present.

"And you're convinced," Pat said, "that Borensen put a high-priced hit out on you to clear a safe path to removing Billy."

I leaned back, folded my arms. "Is that too big a leap for you, old buddy?"

He shook his head. "No. Not at all. You'd have stepped right up to the plate with a big bad bat in your hands, if they murdered that little guy. What kind of shape is he in, anyway?"

"I don't know. He was still out cold when they loaded him in the ambulance."

He frowned. "I don't get it, Mike. Why not leave Billy to us?"

"Let's just say I want him in my protective custody. Think about it. To everybody but you in this department, Billy will be an unfortunate little guy who took some bullets meant for Mike Hammer. How long can you arrange a twenty-four-hour police guard for that?"

"I have *some* influence."

"Okay. So maybe hiding Billy away somewhere isn't necessary. Maybe Billy would be just as well off or better out at Bellevue under police protection. But have you considered I might have another agenda?"

"Such as?"

"Such as someone we both care about."

His eyes flared. "…Velda."

I nodded. "Pat, I want her out of here, away from my side. I'm entering into a very dangerous sort of competition, and I don't want to see her get between me and the next bullet triggered my way."

He was sitting forward. "What do you mean… dangerous competition?"

I told him, in some detail, about last night's phone call from the self-styled greatest of all contract killers. Pat frowned through much of my account, occasionally shaking his head.

"Mike, this guy is worse than just some professional killer. He's a lunatic. A madman."

"Maybe that's why he identifies so closely with me."

"It's not funny, but… I get it, where Velda's concerned. You know she wouldn't leave town or in any way lay low, if you just asked her to, for her safety. You had to give her a job that got her out of harm's way."

"That's right. Pat, I have a suggestion."

"I'm not surprised. What is it?"

"The Martin Foster suicide. That wasn't your case."

"No. That was out on Long Island."

"Well, get whatever you can on it from the local PD out there. Look at everything. Crime scene photos, autopsy report, the works."

He was frowning. "You think Borensen staged it?"

"Very possible. Whether he knew his prospective father-in-law had cancer or not is immaterial. What likely happened is Dick Blazen told Foster the truth about his son-in-law-to-be. Which meant they both had to go."

"Why, because Borensen loves the girl?"

"Well, it would be easy enough to. But you might start with all the money she'll inherit."

"Okay. Can I assume you're working this from your own end?"

I saluted him with my coffee cup. "You know, when I get to the finish line before you—and I *will* get there before you, Pat—how would you like me to drop Borensen right in your lap?"

"And not just kill his ass?"

"Well, no promises, but… yes, if he doesn't pull anything. With his connections, a live Viking might be very useful to your department in putting some worthy mob slobs in the Graybar Hotel."

"Agreed." Pat went deadpan on me. "Now you'll tell me what you want from *me*."

"I assume you weren't working that hit-and-run."

He nodded. "Vehicular homicide isn't my bailiwick."

"Well, round up everything the department has on that crime." I dug in my trenchcoat pocket and found the three slugs from earlier and tossed them on the desk. "And you're going to want these. I dug 'em out of Billy's jacket tonight."

"What the hell did you take them for?" His face got a little red.

"Just wanted to make sure they got to you. Didn't want to leave them to the uniforms, and I planned to get Billy out of there before any plainclothes showed."

The red faded but he was still annoyed. "You're tampering with crime scenes now?"

Really I'd been tampering with crime scenes for a long time, but I said, "You have a decent chain of evidence. I'm an officer of the court, after all, and I preserved material that might have been lost in the shuffle, and instead turned them over to the Captain of Homicide."

"Where would I be without your help?"

I chose to treat that as a rhetorical question, since the answer might embarrass him.

"Look, Pat, assuming Billy is just unconscious, and not in a coma or anything, what we really need on Borensen right now is an ID. You had a police photographer at the Waldorf suite this afternoon. You were interviewing Borensen while your guy was snapping shots. Think it's possible that our suspect might be in the background of one?"

Pat was already reaching for the phone. He got the crime lab and made the request.

After he hung up, he said, "I can see why we need a photo for Billy to identify, since Hy says shots of Borensen are as scarce as honest P.I.'s. But what would make the man feel he had to get rid of Billy? All the bastard needed to do was stay away from Billy's corner. It's not like we'd haul Borensen in for a line-up, or that Billy would turn him up in our mug books. Back when you say he was dealing drugs, Borensen was never even arrested."

"Let me answer you with a question. What do guys who run newsstands do when things get slow?"

Pat shrugged, thinking about it. "Well, they sure don't read the girlie mags. They could get hauled in for that, and it would discourage female customers. And they don't read the funny books, because it just doesn't look good. I suppose they read the papers. Each day's papers."

I gave him a big sunny smile. "And what will be in the paper, one day soon? Not on the sports page. Not on the editorial page. Not in the funnies. But the—"

"Shit," Pat said. "The *society* page."

"Wedding photos," we said.

CHAPTER NINE

As I rolled down the hill in my black Ford, the trio of three-story white-washed stucco buildings, as alike as Monopoly houses, seemed to give off a ghostly glow. Some of that came from security lighting, the rest from moonlight making its way through the misty night.

Valley Vista Sanitarium dominated a dip between rolling hills a few miles south of Newburgh. You had to catch a look at the complex coming down, as the private facility had a seven-foot brick wall and a big wooden gate. The well-spaced-out cluster of buildings on tree-dotted grounds worthy of a country club perched on the Hudson River side, providing patients with a nice view and the hospital with another discreet method for patient arrival and admittance. The river was just a black ribbon with shimmering ivory highlights.

I'd left Pat's office around two a.m. and by three-fifteen was pulling into the short drive up to the imposing Valley Vista gates with their welcoming signs: PRIVATE—KEEP OUT. I got out, .45 in hand, tugged down my hat brim and, leaving the car running, crouched on the driver's side. I was waiting to see if

I'd been right that I hadn't been followed here. For a full five minutes, nobody came in either direction, indicating my abilities to spot a tail remained undiminished by time.

So I put the big gun back in the shoulder rig and went over to use the intercom and announce myself. I'd called ahead and was expected. As the mist's ambitions rose into a light rain, I waited some more, until a beefy orderly in white walked down the much longer, slightly sloping drive to open the gates for me.

The Valley Vista was generally known as a sanitarium for the mentally ill. The middle building was for patients who were receiving therapy after being committed and who would, in time, be released. The building at left was for seriously chronically deranged souls who were humanely store-housed here and would likely never see sunshine on the other side of the brick wall.

The third identical building, at right, was something else again. This was a hospital where patients who needed discreet care could come, and that included the occasional movie star recovering from plastic surgery, a politician drying out, or unsavory types who needed a bullet wound or other illegal-work-related injury tended to without the notification of the authorities.

Only a select few among the citizenry were in the know about the services that third building offered—that it was a cross between Switzerland and a fortress. The orderlies were bruisers and the security team consisted of former Green Berets and other Special Forces types. In its thirty years of existence, Valley Vista had served as neutral territory. Rival gangland bosses were safe here. And it was the one place in this state where Mike Hammer would not kick down a door to get at some mob slob who needed killing.

Or anyway the need for that had never come. Valley Vista stopped short of hiding out wanted men, after all, and had made a very handy resource for Michael Hammer Investigations, from time to time. I'd been here twice recuperating from gunshot wounds that back in the real world would have made me vulnerable. And in my business you sometimes had to hide a witness from the bad guys. Or the cops.

At reception the nurse was giving my ID the onceover twice when Dr. Benson came out from his office and granted me his benediction. Also, his permission not to check my weapon, though I did hang up my raincoat and hat. They could use drying off.

Billy was on the third floor, the doc said, and gave me the room number.

"How serious?" I asked him.

Benson was in his fifties, and had been a medic in the Korean hostilities. He was an average-looking face-in-the-crowd guy except for his prematurely white hair and very light-blue eyes.

"Mr. Batson broke two of his ribs," the doc said. "No sign of internal hemorrhage. When I last looked in, he was still unconscious, but not in a coma. Still, there are often special medical considerations with these little people, and I'd like to keep him here for at least a few days."

I told him that it might be longer. That my friend could be a target for a dangerous but as yet unidentified assassin, and he thanked me for the information. I might have told him someone left their car lights on in the parking lot.

A hospital at night is an eerie place—the beeps and boops of monitoring equipment, the low-key lighting, the nurses floating down corridors like occasional ghosts, plus the usual antiseptic smells. The place was asleep, but fitfully.

In this unique hospital, certain floors had armed guards seated outside doors, big men in light blue uniforms with big revolvers on their hips. Their only concession to the time of night was to sit in wooden chairs as old as the building, and nobody was reading or snacking much less napping. These were men trained in jungles to stay alert in darkness waiting for any snap of a twig to signal an approaching enemy capable of exploding the night into a daylight of orange muzzle discharge and the silence into a symphony of screams and gunfire.

The guard on the door was already on his feet when I turned down the corridor. Just outside the room, he looked me over, but his walkie had already told him to expect me.

He had a naturally sleepy-eyed look, like Robert Mitchum, but he was as alert as hell. Very softly he said, "I believe they're both sleeping, Mr. Hammer."

"Thanks," I said, but I'd have to wake Velda if necessary.

But it wasn't. She was leaned back in a recliner, resting, with the .32 automatic on her lap, but very much awake. Across from her, a light on in the john, its door cracked, provided just enough illumination not to disturb the patient. She had changed into a black jumpsuit—I could see her overnight bag peeking out from behind the chair—and looked like a commando, although I never saw a commando built like that.

Billy, seeming very small, lay on his back in the hospital bed, asleep, breathing hard but not snoring and in no apparent discomfort. They had an IV going.

As soon as I came in, Velda sat up, put the .32 on the table by the recliner, and got to her feet. With a wide smile, she came over into my arms and punched me in the mouth with those pillowy lips of hers.

Then, still in each other's arms, we stared at each other, as if making sure we were both real and not just wishful thinking.

"I've been so worried," she whispered.

Quietly, with a nod toward Billy, I said, "He hasn't woken up yet?"

"No. They've got a morphine drip going, and that may keep him out a while."

I tipped my head toward the door. "We need to talk, kitten."
She nodded.

We made our way to a little waiting area with a couple of chairs and a couch and a low-slung table with the same magazines as the last time I was here, six months ago. Not even the best hospital has a cure for that condition.

I sat in a chair and she sat nearby on the couch. They let you smoke down here and I did. I told Velda I'd filled Pat in and that, after some pissing and moaning, he was onboard with our investigation. Then I got a folded manila envelope out of my inside suit coat pocket.

"Pat rounded up some very interesting art studies for us," I said.

I handed her two crime scene photos from the aftermath of the bridal-shower shooting that clearly showed Borensen talking to Pat in the background.

"The elusive Leif," she said with a smile.

"You keep those for when Billy wakes up."

She shook her head and all that raven hair danced. "I can't believe it's so damn tough to find photos of Borensen."

I shrugged. "I don't think the lack of photos was on purpose. He just wasn't somebody who, despite working in show business, generated much press, or anyway pics. But he knew that marrying Gwen Foster meant wedding photos in the papers, even though the nuptials were going to take place in Hawaii."

"The specialness of that," Velda said, "means even bigger coverage. Anyway, he's poised to go on to bigger things. As the producer, and husband of the star, of a new Broadway musical, he'll be a celebrity himself."

I nodded. "And he couldn't risk Billy seeing any of that splashed all over the papers and other media."

I took out three more photos and handed them to her. Each was an angle on a man slumped over a desktop with a hole in his right temple. His right arm was flung on the desk, his hand palm up, and nearby was a little automatic.

"Smith and Wesson Escort," Velda said. "A .22."

"Small but it did the job. The dead guy is Martin Foster."

"I figured as much. Is that his gun?"

I nodded again. "Registered to him, yes. I'm going to guess he carried it with him for protection in the theater district. He was a well-known, successful man, and a strong personality who wouldn't put up with a mugging or robbery without a fight."

"A strong personality," Velda said, "who killed himself."

"He had lung cancer, and he knew it."

"Leave any note?"

"No."

"No note to his daughter?"

"No. You see any red flags?"

She looked from photo to photo. "I don't think so. Do you, Mike?"

"Not a red flag maybe, but… the fatal wound is side to side, entry wound in one temple, with the expected powder burns and stippling, exit wound through the other temple. To do that, Foster would have to sit down, raise his arm straight, with the elbow out, and fire. A ninety-degree angle."

"That's not impossible."

"Not impossible," I granted. "It might reflect a kind of firing squad mentality. But it's more common, when a suicide sits at a table or desk, for the arm to be at a forty-five degree angle, with the exit wound out the top of the head on the opposite side. Some lean on their elbow and do it."

She shook her head, just a little. "That's not enough to make anything out of, Mike. Nothing says a man like Foster, taking his own life, might not hold his arm straight out. And with his arm on the desk, on its elbow, if he leaned his head against the snout, you'd get the same temple-to-temple effect."

"I know. But it might still be enough to get Pat to look into this deeper. You notice Foster was in his pajamas, and his body wasn't found till the next morning, when Gwen showed up at their beach house."

"I'm not sure I see the significance."

"Well, did he wake up in the middle of the night and kill himself?"

"I'm sure it happens."

"Velda, most depressed types who resort to the Dutch act are well-dressed, almost anticipating their next stop is an open coffin. And Foster doted on his daughter. Would he do this, knowing that she almost *had* to be the one who found him? Would he do that leaving no farewell message? Particularly if the act was due to ill health, not standard despondence."

Velda's narrow-eyed expression said she was buying in. She shook the photos. "So this is *Borensen's* work?"

"Yes. Dick Blazen let Martin Foster know all about Borensen's seedy side, and Foster confronted Borensen. The result is a faked suicide, and a hit-and-run death for Blazen… with the need to get rid of Billy as the only witness capable of identifying him."

"You think Borensen hired that hit-and-run?"

"No. That was Leif himself, all right."

"But, Mike—if our scary friend on the phone the other night was the driver of that hit-and-run vehicle, *he* could be the one who needed Billy dead. After all, he, or one of his people, threw those slugs at Billy tonight, right?"

"Right. But I think Borensen didn't go the hitman route until he figured that *I* needed to be handled. *That* would take a pro. No more do-it-yourself murder. In fact, I'd bet you a marriage license to a buck that this 'suicide' is the work of a professional. The professional who's been sending his minions my way, and who either shot at Billy tonight or had it done."

"No bet," Velda said. "I think you're right. I think Borensen handled Blazen himself, then the fallout was something he couldn't handle. Possibly his mob friends stepped in and ordered him to go with a professional, here on out."

I grinned at my smart cookie of a partner. "Velda, that's a very good read. I should have thought of that."

Her expression melted and she reached out and touched my unshaven face. "Mike… you look beat, darling. You have to get some sleep. You want to camp out in Billy's room? We'll have a rollaway sent up."

I stretched. "No, I better get back to the city. I'll grab some sleep and get back at it."

I looked in on Billy and he was still off in a drug-induced Happy Land.

"You call me when he's had a look at those crime scene photos," I whispered, as I walked her back to the recliner. "With Billy's ID, Pat may be able to move on Borensen."

"What's *your* next move?"

"Getting to Borensen before Pat does."

She shook her head. "And what? Kill him?"

"No," I said. "At least not until I beat the name of his hitman out of him."

"Leif's a big guy, Mike."

"Bigger they are, the harder—"

"They fall, yes," she said with a smirk, "I know, everybody knows."

Half-way out the door I said, "I was going to say, the harder I kick their teeth in."

The rain got out of the sun's way and by the time I got back to Manhattan, dawn was clawing its way up and around the towering glass-and-steel tombstones. I left the Ford in the parking garage, but walking to the elevator, I felt an uneasiness settle in over me like a flu-driven chill. So many cars, and no one but me around. Even the attendant off duty. My footsteps were hollow little things, tiny signs of life in a dead cavernous space.

Fear is an old friend to me. I embrace it. I grin at it. I know how to turn it into energy, into alertness, into big goddamn trouble for the other guy.

But right now the emptiness around me as I walked spooked me bad. Was it fear? Not really. But a guy as good at killing as my phone caller claimed to be could pop up out of anywhere and plunk me into the next life...

...leaving Velda alone, to fend for herself.

I knew if any woman could do that, really could fend for her own self, Velda was that woman. But the idea of danger, of death, hovering over her without me there to stop it, was fueling the fearful uneasiness that was giving me chill-like shakes.

That hospital, Valley Vista, was a citadel not easily stormed, but it could be done. Any fort can be breached, any soldier can go down under another soldier's gun. And if something happened to me, wouldn't Velda leave Billy behind and go out on some crazy-ass revenge trip like... like I would?

But nobody popped out from behind a parked car to pop me, and I rode the elevator alone up to the third floor and my apartment at the end of the hall, went in with the .45 ready, and found the place empty.

You're paranoid, a voice in my head said derisively. Then another voice said, *You're not paranoid when they're really out to get you, Hammer.*

"But what are you," I asked the room, "if you're hearing voices?"

The .45 went on my nightstand and I got out of my suit and tie, but that was as far as I made it before collapsing onto the bed into something deep and mercifully dreamless.

The phone woke me.

I fumbled for it. "Yeah?"

"Pat," the phone said. "You asleep?"

"Not now."

The clock radio said 1:10 and a high-up sun was filtering through the windows.

"Well, some of us keep regular hours," he said. "You know, like working from eight in the morning till two the next morning? It's Sunday, chum, but no day of rest for either of us. Wipe the sleep from your eyes, because I found out something that will interest you."

Wide awake now, I sat up, stuffed a pillow behind me and leaned back against the headboard. "Go, man, go."

"Borensen owns a vehicle that matches the one your friend Billy described. According not only to Billy but several other witnesses—who did not see the driver well but did see the hit-and-run go down—the vehicle was a dark green late-model Cadillac… with no license plates."

"That says premeditation right there, removing the plates. Homicide by hit-and-run, intentional."

"Yes it does. Now here's the really interesting thing. The same day that Richard Blazen got run down by a dark green Caddy, Leif Borensen reported his car stolen."

"Before or after the hit-and-run?"

"After. Not much after, though."

"He probably pulled over and removed those license plates before he did the deed. Then ducked in somewhere, a parking garage maybe, and put them back on."

"No argument."

"Was the 'stolen' car ever found?"

"Nope," Pat said. "I'm guessing it never will be."

"Leif probably turned it over to some chop shop crew. Or left it on the street with the keys in and let the laws of human nature do his dirty work for him."

"Mike, if we can get that ID out of Billy, we've got the real beginnings of a case against Borensen here. So how about you letting your tax dollars work for you? Tell me where you're keeping Billy. And then stay out of this one, okay?"

I hung up on him.

A hot shower and a shave under the spray turned me human again. Toweling off, I caught my reflection in the mirror and saw a patchwork of healed bullet and blade wounds and other residual scar tissue. The Frankenstein monster had nothing on me.

In my jockey shorts and T-shirt, I got into a fresh white shirt, then slipped on the shoulder holster. I dripped a few drops of oil into the .45's slide mechanism and checked the clip before easing the rod in. Safety off, one in the chamber. When a hired gun is on your tail, certain precautions need to be sacrificed.

I picked out a clean suit, cut to conceal the weapon of course, a medium gray number that would look pretty sharp with a darker gray tie.

After all, I was calling on millions of dollars and wanted to look my Sunday best.

Outside the Blue Ribbon, where I'd caught up with lunch, I flagged a cab, getting a wide-eyed look from the Puerto Rican driver who must have read the papers or maybe watched the local TV news, because his reaction said he not only recognized me, but knew what had happened to another recent cabbie who'd pulled over for me.

To his credit, he just took the address, nodded, and got going, through light traffic. Like the song says, the big city was taking a nap. Before long the cab pulled up at the fancy Park Avenue apartment building across from which Central Park, courtesy of a sunny Sunday, was showing a good time to couples, families and tourists.

Of course, immediately opposite us was the stone wall where a shooter, not long ago, had perched.

The cabbie said, "Isn't this where...?"

"Yup. Right here."

"*Ea diablo!* I *would* have to draw Mike Hammer for a fare."

I already had the rider's side rear door open, and handed him up a ten. "You're a good man, *panna*. Keep the change."

He grinned at me, then at the sawbuck, and got instant amnesia about what had happened to his fellow hackie.

"You welcome in my cab *any* time, Mr. Hammer!"

The doorman in his comic-opera livery recognized me, too, and gave me a nod and a "Good afternoon, sir."

I told the guy I was just dropping by to see how the Borensens were doing after that nasty business at the Waldorf-Astoria the other day.

He gave me a look that said people didn't just "drop by" this kind of apartment building, no matter how well-meaning.

"You'll have to phone up there," I said, "and make sure I'm welcome."

That he could handle, and he stepped inside to use the house phone on the entryway wall. I couldn't hear him on the other side of the glass, but he was nodding as he listened.

Soon he came out, opened the door for me, gave me the respectful head lowering routine, and said, "Miss Foster said to go on up, Mr. Hammer."

I nodded to him and went in and crossed the marble-floored ballroom of a lobby to the bank of elevators. When I stepped off into the apartment's entry area, the rush of its waterfall sounding like somebody forgot to turn off a big spigot, Gwen was already waiting for me.

This was neither the pop-art girl in red nor the bride-to-be in a yellow cocktail dress. This was the kind of fresh-faced collegiate type that made a high school dropout sorry.

Her honey-blonde hair was swept back off her forehead and brushed the shoulders of a white turtle-neck sweater interrupted by the perk of perfect handfuls on the way down to low-slung gray trousers with a wide black leather belt with a big buckle that would have looked just right on a pirate. She wore dark brown moccasins with no socks, and her only make-up was some pink gloss on lips that, years before she was born, would have been characterized as bee-stung.

Gwen Foster was a doll, the living variety, and she sure as hell deserved better than Leif Borensen.

She bounced up to me and gripped both of my hands as if I were a favorite uncle and gave me a lovely smile, the blue eyes catching light and tossing it around. "Mike… so *wonderful* to see you."

"I just wanted to check up on you and Leif. See how you two were doing in the aftermath of that bridal shower interruptus."

Gwen rolled her eyes. "I'm just glad you and Miss Sterling were there."

She accompanied me into and across the high-ceilinged foyer with its marble floor and crystal chandelier. Her voice echoed a little now. Our footsteps, too.

"I admit I had some trouble sleeping that first night, Mike, but I've been fine since. I just got back from brunch with some of my girl friends, who were there at the Waldorf, and assured me it was a shower no one would *ever* forget."

When she followed this with some brittle laughter, it seemed a little forced to me. But at least she wasn't freaked out over the incident.

"I think Leif is probably in the study," she said, as we went down the landing strip of a hallway with its wall-hugging antiques and museum's worth of pricey paintings. Once again she looped her arm in mine. Her perfume had a sparkling brightness about it and I recognized it as one Velda had been wearing lately—*Oh! De London*.

"I just got back a little while ago from my luncheon," she said, as we neared the door. "I know Leif will be pleased to see you. We owe you some money, don't we?"

"That's not why I'm here. I just wanted to check up on you, you know, since that shower didn't go exactly as planned."

Or had it gone exactly *as Borensen had planned it?*

I said, "But I do have some business matters I need to go over with Mr. Borensen. Much as your company would surely help relieve the boredom, I'd suggest you take a pass."

I really didn't want her there when I spoke to her husband-to-be. I hoped the future bride would be somewhere else in this vast apartment, and far enough away not to hear me interrogate the future groom by beating the living shit out of him.

She didn't need to learn, so brutally, that the man she loved had murdered her father by way of a cold-blooded staged suicide. And there was always the possibility that Borensen, faced with my knowledge of his wrongdoing, might go for a gun, giving me the pleasure of blowing the insides of his head all over some very expensive shelved books, though their leather bindings should clean off nicely.

No, none of it was anything I wanted Gwen to see. I'm just too considerate a guy for that.

"Business talk bores me," she said, hand on the knob. "So I'll leave you two to it. Let me just check on Leif and make sure he's not in the middle of anything."

She slipped into the study, leaving the door ajar, and perhaps three seconds later came the scream.

High-pitched and bloodcurdling, turning sharp and shrill as it resounded off the high ceiling of the library-like room.

I went in fast, with my .45 in my fist. But almost immediately I stuffed the weapon back under my arm, because it wouldn't be needed.

At a small writing desk in the far corner, Leif Borensen, in a brown terry-cloth bathrobe, sat slumped with his head to one side, in a pool of congealing blood, displaying the small powder-burned hole in his temple, his hand, palm up, limply near a small .22 handgun—a Smith and Wesson Escort.

CHAPTER TEN

Pat stood with his hands on his hips and surveyed the death scene, close enough to tap Borensen on his shoulder. I was sitting across the big book-lined room on one of the comfortable brown-leather chairs where I'd first spoken with my late client. I had an ankle on a knee and was smoking a cigarette. I'd already had my own good close look, waiting for Pat to get here.

I figured correctly that he'd be home by now, so the way I called the crime in was to phone him at his apartment. I knew he wouldn't want any other homicide dick catching this one. As it was, he'd beat everybody else here, but now a small army of NYPD lab boys awaited access in the vast hallway, as well as a photographer and three plainclothes guys from the Homicide Division. Uniforms were here and there, standing just outside the study and posted variously, in the waterfall entry area by the elevators for example, and downstairs keeping the liveried doorman company. A policewoman, plainclothes, was sitting with the distraught Gwen in the kitchen.

Pat turned and frowned at me. "Bored, Mike?"

For a guy who'd probably collapsed on his couch a few hours

ago after one of his longer days, he looked pretty fresh. Crisp blue suit and blue-and-red tie, freshly shaved, hair brushed back. And from where I sat, you couldn't see his bloodshot eyes.

"No," I said. "I just know when somebody is telling me to go screw myself."

He frowned at that and walked over to the central area of chairs on the Oriental rug. "You shouldn't smoke."

"Yeah, that's what Velda says."

"No, I mean at a crime scene. Put it out."

I put it out on an ashtray on the glass-topped coffee table that displayed *Playbills* from various Martin Foster productions. Pat sat opposite me with that coffee table between us. He was frowning, staring at me with his gray-blue eyes. Bloodshot gray-blue eyes.

"Mind explaining," he said, "why you think someone is telling you to go screw yourself?"

I shrugged. I felt nicely comfortable in the over-stuffed chair. "It's not just me being told that. You're getting the big 'up yours,' too."

"Tell me."

"You want me to spell it out?"

"Yes."

"That's no suicide."

"You make it as phony."

"And so do you, Pat."

"So what is it, then?"

"Well, it's homicide, of course. But a cute one—a replication of another phony suicide. The killer staged this not in order to fool anybody, but to laugh his ass off at us. The body is positioned just like Foster's. The wound is identical—that same ninety-degree angle that has the bullet going straight through one temple and out the other. The weapon is not only the same caliber but the identical make and model. No suicide note. Informal attire, in Foster's case pajamas, in Borensen's a bathrobe. He isn't even wearing slippers."

"Why would a killer *do* this?"

Some edge colored my tone. "You aren't listening, Pat. Maybe you hear me, but you are not goddamn listening. The killer is thumbing his nose at us."

His voice had grown very quiet. "And you *know* who that killer is?"

"I do. I can't give you his name and his address or even his description, but I know who and what we're dealing with here."

He shifted in his comfy chair. "Are you trying to tell me we've been looking at the wrong suspect? That Borensen *didn't* drive that hit-and-run vehicle? That he *didn't* hire your contract killing?"

I shook my head. "You shouldn't work such long hours, buddy. It's softening your skull. Borensen was guilty of all those things, *and* Foster's rigged suicide. There's some question as to whether he did the latter himself or hired it done, but otherwise… Pat, I can't do any more of your thinking for you on this unless you're prepared to put me on the city payroll."

He put an elbow on a knee and ran a hand over his face. The poor bastard was exhausted. He was caught up in a case so confusing and convoluted, it was getting to him. All the way.

Then his hand dropped away and his expression said he got the drift. Belatedly, but I knew that detective's mind of his was in there somewhere.

"This is your late-night caller," he said, eyes wide, a fist chest high. "This is the work of the hitman Borensen hired, only now that we're really digging into the case, he's tying off loose ends."

"Give the man a cigar," I said. "Of course, it's tough to go after a contract killer when the brains of the guy who hired him are splattered on a desk."

"It's more than tying off loose ends, though." Pat's eyes may have been bloodshot, but they were alive with thought now. "This is part of his crazy desire to pit himself against you, Mike. It's his sick game, a contest, killer against killer. And going to the trouble of handling Borensen's 'suicide' in a way that *shouts* that it's been staged is... man, it's crazy."

"But with method in the madness," I said.

Pat sat forward and the eyes were cold now, hard. "And you're right, Mike, he's telling us both to go screw ourselves. I'm sure you'll deal with it in some colorful and quasi-legal fashion, but me? I'm treating this as a homicide scene. Our big shot assassin will have screwed up somewhere, and we'll nail him."

I got to my feet. Shortly I would not be wanted here.

"I'm not so sure he screwed up anywhere, old buddy," I told him. "This one is a pro among pros—a bat-shit crazy one, maybe, but a pro."

And as for nailing him, that was Hammer's job.

I joined Gwen in the kitchen, which was white with black touches, modern as tomorrow, and predictably spacious. She sat at a Formica gray-topped table for four, which I figured she and her father (and later her fiancé) had rarely if ever used. An informal dining room adjacent was surely where rich people in an apartment like this would take their meals.

The policewoman, with the build of a prison guard but a pleasant face that conveyed sympathy, was seated next to Gwen. In front of both were coffee cups, their dark liquid untouched.

I sat down, giving the policewoman a look and head toss that said I wanted some privacy with the girl. The policewoman, who knew I was Captain Chambers' crony, merely nodded back and stepped outside the kitchen.

Gwen's hands were folded, clutching the latest tissue from a box the policewoman had provided, and she was staring at them with eyes raccooned with runny mascara. Otherwise she remained a lovely young woman in sweater and slacks, blonde hair touching her shoulders, a young beauty perfect enough for a Breck ad.

I touched those hands and, after a few beats, she looked up at me.

"Why?" she asked.

That was the first question, the only question, for a loved one to ask after an unexpected suicide. But the "why" here was a complicated and nasty one. This kid was dazed, staggered by the shock. She would have to know what this was about. She deserved that much and more.

But was now the time?

Pat and the lab boys would be here for hours. It didn't matter that it was Sunday. Soldiers do battle every day of the week. Borensen's body would be gone before the cops were, and because Pat viewed this as a homicide, that body was evidence

149

and morgue-bound, with no pressing need for her to deal with funeral arrangements.

Of course, that hadn't occurred to her, not yet.

She looked at me with the blue eyes large and ringed with black, and hurt and rage shimmered there and she gripped my hands now, and shouted, "*Why*, goddamnit? *Why?*"

So I told her.

I warned her first that she would not like what I had to say. And she found a ghastly little smile as she told me she could not imagine things could get any worse.

She was wrong.

But I told her anyway. I put it together like a story, the worst once-upon-a-time ever, starting with Borensen's criminal background, from drug dealing to money laundering. I figured if she couldn't grasp that, or refused to, I wouldn't have to go on with my story.

When I'd completed that portion, however, she said quietly, "I've heard this before."

That surprised me. "You have?"

She nodded. "My father told me he'd learned all of that about Leif. He didn't say where he'd got it, but I assumed he'd hired detectives to… he didn't hire *you* to do that, did he, Mike? You did say you knew my father."

"No, he didn't hire me. I believe your father learned about your fiancé's criminal history from an old-time publicity agent who was writing his memoirs. Did you believe what your dad told you?"

She swallowed, shook her head. "No. Or, anyway, I thought he was exaggerating things. Mike, it may sound terrible, but a lot of people in theater, in show business, do use drugs. I see it all the time. It's not my thing, but… that a struggling actor like Leif would have to have some way to make money on the side, that didn't surprise me. And as far as what you call 'money laundering,' a lot of funds from shady circles back plays and movies. I'm young, Mike, but I'm not a child."

"Understood. Did you ever talk to Leif about this?"

She shook her head again. "No. I thought it was a kind of… invasion of privacy. And after my father was gone, I didn't feel like getting into it."

That was a hell of a thing, wasn't it? Borensen had been afraid Foster would poison his daughter against her fiancé with the lurid tale of a sordid past, and so the prospective son-in-law either murdered his prospective father-in-law by way of a faked suicide, or hired it done.

And it had been completely unnecessary.

"I'm not an innocent, Mr. Hammer," she said, chin up, her smile a wrinkled little thing. "Working as an actress, a singer, even with the kind of pedigree I had thanks to Daddy, well… you meet a lot of different kinds of people in that world. You encounter a lot of different kinds of things."

So I pressed on, telling her how her fiancé had used his car as a murder weapon, running down that publicity agent.

That turned her white as a blister.

"I thought the car had been stolen," she said.

"So did the police," I said.

I continued, telling her there had been a witness to the hit-and-run, a harmless Munchkin who ran a newsstand, but Leif needed him dead, too… only this witness was a friend of mine, and Leif feared my involvement. I had a reputation of settling scores where my friends were concerned. So the man she'd loved had taken steps to have me killed, as a preventative measure.

Gwen had seen the papers, of course, and knew all about the killer who'd confronted me in my office. She knew, too, that after I'd conferred with Leif about the bridal shower gig, I'd been shot at down on the street, and an innocent cab driver had been killed.

She said, "If you're right, that means Leif used my bridal... *my* bridal shower to set up a bogus robbery, all for another attempt on your life? Endangering me and every one of my guests?"

"Yes," I said.

She folded her arms to herself and shivered, though it wasn't cold. "I wish... I wish I could argue against that. I really do. But you are very convincing, Mike."

I touched her sleeve. "You okay, kid?"

"Feeling a little sick, that's all."

But it wasn't till I told her about the recent attempt on Billy's life that she finally lurched over to the sink and threw up.

So much for the Sunday brunch.

The cops cleared out around eight p.m. In the big echoing marble-floored entryway, Pat told me that the entrance to the library had been sealed and I wasn't to go in there nosing around. I nodded like that meant anything.

"How's Miss Foster taking it?" he asked.

"All right, considering I let her in on everything."

He frowned. "You think that's wise?"

"She has a right to know. She *wanted* to know." I nodded toward the nearby stairway. "She took a sleeping pill and's resting in a guest room upstairs. I'll check in with her before I go."

He was frowning, worried for the girl. "No relatives locally to sit with her?"

"She says not."

"A place like this surely has household staff."

"Not live-in, she says, and anyway today's their day off."

He sighed. "You better get the name of some friends of hers you can try, to see if anybody can come be with her. She's been through the damn mill."

"Yes she has," I said. "You'll be back tomorrow, with a fresh team?"

He nodded. "Everybody in the building has to be questioned, from residents to personnel. There's a super with a staff of two, although only he was working today. My guess is our guy slipped in the building when the door was open while the super was taking out trash or some such."

"The assassin had probably been here before, to meet with his client, and knew his way around. Gwen doesn't know how lucky she is."

"How's that?"

"Think about it, Pat. If she'd been here, he might have taken her out, too. On the other hand, she regularly has Sunday brunch with friends, and a pro killer would do his due diligence, and know that. Killer came in, caught a freshly showered Borensen in his bathrobe and walked him down to the study, either at gunpoint or on a pretense of urgent business. Have your forensics experts look for traces of soapy water on the carpet in there, and the upstairs hallway and stairs."

He grinned a little. "I'd almost think you were a detective, Mike."

Then he patted me on the shoulder, and was the last of the cop crew to leave.

Upstairs in that darkened guest room, I went over and sat on the edge of the bed. Outside, the sunny day was over and the sky was rumbling with the threat of some real rain.

I whispered, "Are you sleeping?"

She sat up, the blonde hair finally mussed. "I *was* napping... I just woke up. Did I hear those police people leaving?"

"You did. Can you give me the name and number of a girl friend or two, who I can call so you can have some company tonight?"

She shook her head. "No, I'll be fine. I don't want to have to talk to anybody."

"Understood. Look, I'll be glad to camp out here. I just might be able to find a spare room someplace."

She actually smiled a little, and touched my arm. "No, I'll be fine, Mike. I'm a big girl."

"Not really. You're a slip of thing, and I've got ties older than you. I'll be glad to stand guard."

"You think I need guarding?"

"Truthfully... no. And since I'm somebody's favorite target right now, maybe I'm putting you in danger just being here. Maybe I should go."

She nodded, touched my face, then rolled over, her back to me as I went out. I was out by the waterfall waiting for the elevator when that electrically controlled door hissed open and she was standing poised in the doorway, hair every which way, her face washed of all make-up, in just a T-shirt and sheer panties, the former poked by the tips of pert breasts, the latter revealing a shade of blonde only slightly darker than her head of askew hair.

"*Mike!* Please stay! I don't want to be alone tonight."

She's young, Hammer, a voice said in my head. *And it would be a shitty thing to do to Velda. And this kid's vulnerable right now, really hurting. You'd be taking advantage, you lowlife prick.*

Silently I told the voice, *Who says I'm going to do anything but comfort the kid? You have a dirty damn mind.*

The elevator came and I ignored it. She held out her hand and I took it. We went up the stairs to the guest room. She'd said she couldn't stand to be in her own bed, where she'd been with Borensen many times, or the master bedroom, where the couple had moved after her father's death.

The room was dark. She got under the covers. I got out of my suit coat, tie, and shoes, but left everything else on, and lay down on top of the covers. Outside the sky laughed deep in its throat at me and then a downpour came, so loud we had to really talk to communicate. Whispering wouldn't quite cut it.

"Someone came in this place today," she said, dread in her voice, "and killed Leif—that really *happened?* Someone warped enough to mimic my daddy's death? Just to send you a kind of… a kind of sick message?"

"I'm afraid so."

"I know a lot of bad people, Mike. The theater has a lot of good, generous people in it, but also jealous ones, back-biters, producers and directors who want sex before giving you a part, liars, cheats, thieves, and you run into what you think is bad behavior, all the time, when you're an actor. But this man is *really* bad, isn't he? Not just awful, but *evil*."

"Yes."

"Will you stop him?"

"Yes."

"Everything wrong that Leif did, I still… it's horrible, Mike, but I still haven't stopped loving him. My head knows he was terrible, but my heart can't accept it. He killed my father, you say."

"Or hired it done."

"That's… unspeakable. A betrayal that you can't even imagine."

I could imagine it. A woman once said she loved me, and accepted my proposal of marriage, and offered herself to me naked and lovely while reaching behind me for a gun in a potted plant.

In the darkness, nearby but a hundred miles away, her voice came: "Did he ever love me, do you think? Really love me? Or was I just someone he *used*… like he used my father?"

"Hard to know, honey. He may have loved you in his way."

"His way?"

"Some people, the really evil ones, go through life as actors. Not your kind of actor, no, but actors who don't have certain human feelings, so they watch and learn and imitate those feelings. They're aliens moving among us, these people."

"…Would you do me a favor, Mike?"

"Anything, honey."

"Just… get undressed and get under the covers with me. I need to be held. Would you do that? And just hold me? Just make me feel not… alone."

I stripped down to my skivvies and got in bed with the kid. She nestled under my arm and slipped an arm across my middle, her head against my chest.

"I wouldn't be so hard to love, would I, Mike? I mean, really love?"

"No. It'd be easy."

She lifted her head up and kissed me. It was tender, soft, yet electric. As if confirming that, the room strobed with lightning through the sheer curtains. The sky roared like a roused beast, and the rain kept drumming down, relentless but rhythmic.

She slipped out of bed and went to the window and looked out. I turned away from her. I couldn't do this. It was wrong. She was a kid who had a thing for father figures and I wasn't going to take advantage. She was wounded and I would not, goddamnit, take advantage.

I turned back over to tell her I thought I should go. Somewhere between the bed and the window, she'd lost her T-shirt and panties. At least I thought so—the room was very dark.

Then lightning strobed and there she was, every bit of her there in the stark white light the sky provided between roars, so slender yet shapely, her back to me, the globes of her bottom high and firm and round, the dimples so deep their dark hollows survived through the flash of light. When the strobing was over, she was just a lovely shape, barely distinct when she turned to me.

"I need this, Mike," she said. "It'll be just this once."

"No," I said. "Take a couple more sleeping pills and get some rest. This thing has you ragged."

The sky strobed again and for an instant she was an ivory

statue, a goddess with high superbly shaped breasts, not large, just perfect, and a sleek body, her belly flat but gently muscular, her sleek, supple legs apart just enough for the curly triangle to offer a glimpse of delights I knew I should not sample.

I got out of bed, intending to get into my clothes, but my interest in her obvious.

Her eyes widened appreciatively and then she did something I didn't expect her to be able to, under the circumstances—she laughed. She came quickly over and shoved me on the bed. Then I heard her fumbling in a nightstand drawer and moments later I felt the rubber sliding down and I thought, *No, she* isn't *an innocent.*

Then she rode me, slow and sweet and finally building to something not sweet at all, but just as wonderful as the sight of her when the lightning strobes showed her to me, little snapshots of youthful female perfection, and a head of blonde hair that swung like a mane, and a face so beautiful and so blissful, as the act cancelled out anything else in her mind, sadness, betrayal, it was all gone, for those minutes.

As for the voices in my head, nobody bitched.

She'd told me the help arrived at six-thirty a.m., so I got up around five, and had a shower, while she continued to sleep. Though Pat had the study sealed, I thought there might be a door from the second floor onto the upper level of the book stacks, where I could get in without tipping my hand. I was right.

Within moments I made my way to the desk where Borensen had died. On the desktop, a pool of crusty dried blood, black with hardly any red highlights, bore the imprint of where his head had fallen. No attempt at a chalk outline had been made, though an X in a circle indicated where the gun had been, and the chair was circled in chalk to show its position. Still, I felt free to seat myself in that chair of honor, and—fingerprints having already been taken—began looking through the desk drawers.

As I suspected, Borensen had made the desk his own, and the only sign that Martin Foster had once sat and worked here were letters that had "cc:" to Borensen, correspondence relating to the musical production they were planning to mount together. This included a number of letters from Johnny Mercer himself and the Maxwell Anderson estate, for the rights to the *Star Wagon* play.

Finally I came across some banking materials—a savings book, a checkbook with register, and an envelope of monthly statements. These showed that Leif Borensen was keeping a quarter of a million dollars and change in a savings account at a Manhattan bank.

That didn't surprise me. He hadn't gone after Gwen with marrying money in mind. This was about "marrying" a theatrical impresario whose name and reputation would lift Borensen to a higher level—that and aligning himself with a gifted young performer in Gwen.

I did find one interesting, possibly suggestive item. Make that "items." Borensen had made out two checks, $25,000 each, to the Institute for Neurological Disease. Was Borensen a closet philanthropist?

I looked for the cancelled checks and found them. They were

deposited in a bank in Cold Spring in upstate New York. So the institute wouldn't be tough to track.

Gwen was just waking up when I slipped into the guest room to say my goodbyes.

"You're leaving?" she asked sleepily. You know a woman is beautiful when she wakes up beautiful.

"Yes. You don't want me here when the help shows."

She frowned at the onset of reality. "Oh, dear. I'll need to tell them what happened...."

"It'll be in all the papers. I wouldn't tell them anything beyond that Mr. Borensen seems to have taken his own life. They'll be sympathetic and leave it at that."

That calmed her. "Mike... last night was... thank you. I needed to be close to someone. I just want you to know..."

"Honey," I said, leaning in, "I know. A young Broadway star and a broken-down old private eye have no future together. It was a one-time thing for both of us. But I'll never forget it."

She reached herself up and gave me a little kiss. "You may be old but you're not broken-down."

"That's half a compliment, anyway. Listen, did you ever hear of something called the Institute for Neurological Disease? I think it's upstate somewhere."

"Actually, yes. It's a research facility. I was involved in a telethon for them, a year or so ago. They've made some real breakthroughs."

"Did you know that Leif gave fifty thousand dollars to them?"

She shrugged. "No, I didn't. I didn't know he had any interest in that particular cause. Really, I don't remember him ever giving to any kind of charity. Is that significant?"

I gave her a quick kiss of my own. "Honey, in my world, fifty grand is *always* significant."

CHAPTER ELEVEN

An hour and a half north of Manhattan, Cold Spring was a hamlet of maybe fifteen hundred at the deepest point of the Hudson, a step into the past with its idyllic setting and downtown of well-preserved nineteenth-century buildings, well-served by a sunny Indian summer day. They made rifles and cannons here, a century ago, but now a battery factory kept the place afloat.

At odds with the old-timey nature of the village, the Institute for Neurological Disease—just outside Cold Spring—was a modern, low-slung glass-and-brick sprawl that might have been a grade school or a power-and-water facility. Somehow it seemed a misnomer against the majesty of nearby Storm King Mountain.

I hadn't called ahead. Phoning the information desk at the New York Public Library got me everything I needed, including the name of the Institute's founder—Dr. Clayton R. Beech.

I pulled the Ford into a parking lot with perhaps fifty other cars, and strolled into a doctor's waiting room of a lobby and directly to the nurse/receptionist's desk. The nurse was a pleasant-featured Nordic type in her fifties who still looked like a good time. She gave me a professionally polite smile that took the edge off the obvious confusion of someone who rarely dealt with walk-ins.

I took off my hat and gave her my own polite smile. "I wonder if Dr. Beech might be in. I'd like to see him."

That seemed to amuse her, but she tried not to show it. Very blue eyes on this matronly gal.

"Sir, Dr. Beech seldom sees *anyone*—he's extremely hands-on in our research here—and when he *does* see someone, it's by appointment only, usually months in advance. If you could tell me the nature of your call, we might be able to arrange something early next year."

I put on an unhappy face. "That's disappointing." I sighed dramatically.

"Well, I'm sorry, sir."

"It's just that I was here about a fifty-thousand dollar donation."

She reached for the phone.

In five minutes, my hat in my lap, I was seated in an office of modest size, decorated only with diplomas and a calendar with flying-geese artwork. The furnishings, including a wall of filing cabinets lined up behind me like a row of soldiers, were coldly modern, like the facility.

But Dr. Beech exuded a warmth that came across immediately, unless that was something he worked up for prospective donors.

Around five ten, in his mid-sixties, bald up top but with black-and-gray sideburns that developed into a well-trimmed beard, the doctor stopped to shake my hand—and get my name—before settling in behind his desk. In the expected white smock with a dark blue bow tie, he had the build of a linebacker, gone slump-shouldered, and the wire-framed glasses of a professor, bifocals.

At his back, and the only impressive thing about this space, was a picture window on to a gymnasium-size laboratory where dozens of other white-smocked professionals were seated and sometimes standing at a row of vertically arranged benches arrayed with test tubes, beakers, flasks, Bunsen burners, heavy-duty microscopes, and sophisticated gizmos beyond my recognition.

Dr. Beech noticed I was looking past him and smiled, tenting his fingers, elbows leaned on a desk where everything was tidy, all papers stacked, even framed family photos arranged symmetrically.

"It's one-way glass," he said, in a bland mid-range voice. "They never know when I'm watching."

I grinned. "At least it's not constant, like Big Brother."

He might have been offended by that crack, but he wasn't. Or, again, maybe he cut potential big-money donors some slack.

"Michael Hammer," he said, tasting the words, eyes narrowing behind the round lenses of his glasses. "I've heard that name but I'm afraid I can't place it."

"I have a rather successful private investigation agency in Manhattan. There's been media coverage now and then."

Now he was nodding, and smiling. "Ah, yes. You're a well-known figure, considered notorious in some circles. I believe you've been in some rather hair-raising scrapes over the years."

"Scrapes and escapes, yes."

He was trying to process that. I was well-known, so did that mean I had money? That I was a success? I was famous—okay, infamous—as someone who had killed but stayed within the limits of the law. Did that mean I felt guilty, and wanted to kick some dough in to a good cause? Help some people live, instead of die?

"I know you're a busy man, Doctor. But I only know very generally what you do here. Could you explain it in more detail, but still keep it in layman's terms?"

The smile blossomed wide in the black-and-gray beard. "Certainly, Mr. Hammer. We have been working on cures and vaccines for numerous neurological conditions and disorders. We've enjoyed great success, virtually wiping out several such diseases in the thirty years this institute has been in existence."

"That's wonderful. Very admirable, sir."

He nodded, proud but not smug. "For several years we've put the lion's share of our focus on a rare but debilitating disease called Phasger's Syndrome, named for the first known patient to display the symptoms. That was in 1918."

"What *are* the symptoms, Doctor?"

He flipped a hand. "They are actually quite mild, Mr. Hammer, initially. So mild that those who've contracted the disease often don't know it until it's too late. The victim has a strong sensation of a bitter taste, and the constant scent of ashes, followed by mild muscular aches not unlike the flu. In these early stages, we can already cure Phasger's, and we are frankly on the brink of a total cure."

The quiet pride in his voice said he could picture the Nobel Prize for Medicine on his wall right now, between the diplomas and the ducks.

"When you say 'brink,' Doctor—how close are you?"

The linebacker shoulders shrugged. "Five years. A year? It's impossible to say, as a breakthrough at any given time can change everything. But I'm confident that ten years from now, Phasger's

Syndrome will be a remnant of the past, like polio."

"Impressive." I gestured toward the small army of research scientists. "How do you manage such feats? I would imagine the costs are staggering."

"They are," he said, "yet we get no government funding, and are wholly independent in that fashion. We survive on grants and gifts from corporations, charitable groups, and of course…" He gestured toward me with a smile. "…individuals."

I smiled back at him. "The kindness of strangers, somebody said. You mentioned the early symptoms, Doctor. What does full-blown Phasger's Syndrome develop into?"

His expression turned grave. "Something quite terrible. Every facet of the nervous system attacks the patient. The pain is excruciating and constant. It is resistant to the most potent pain medications. Something like morphine, in this context, is akin to giving aspirin to a migraine sufferer. Within a year a patient is bedridden, and must be fed intravenously. Speech is distorted to the eventual point of incomprehensibility. There is frequent bleeding from every orifice, requiring regular transfusions. The gums decay, and the teeth rot and fall out. Blindness gradually occurs within the first six months. These poor wretches… excuse my melodramatic phrasing… are prisoners in their own bodies, bodies that are declaring war on themselves."

"Damn."

He flipped the other hand. "So you can see why we work so diligently, around the clock, to eradicate this cruel killer. And you can see why we are so grateful to those, like yourself, who are willing to step up and contribute to this important work."

"I'm sure you are."

The smile blossomed even bigger. "And I must say, Mr. Hammer, that the figure you mentioned to my nurse is an impressive one. From a private individual, particularly one with no history of Phasger's in the family, such a donation is rare indeed. Fifty thousand dollars will go a very long way in this research."

"I'm afraid your nurse misunderstood, Doctor."

"Oh?"

"As you know, I'm a private investigator. And I'm here to ask about a fifty-thousand dollar contribution someone made to your institute. Actually, *two* twenty-five-thousand dollar contributions."

He drew back in his chair, sucking in breath, agape. Well, why not? Hadn't I sucker-punched him?

From my inside suit coat pocket, I withdrew the two cancelled checks and I put them in front of him. "Leif Borensen made these generous donations, both in recent months. Take a look."

Frowning, he did so, without touching them. Maybe he was afraid of catching something. "I do remember these."

"What do you remember about Leif Borensen?"

"Why, nothing."

"He wasn't a patient? Or don't you have patients here?"

His eyes and nostrils flared. "Do I have to tell you, Mr. Hammer, that patient confidentiality—"

So they did treat sufferers, or experiment on them.

"Doc, you already said you didn't remember anything about Borensen. Can you confirm he *wasn't* a patient?"

He thought about that so long, I thought his beard might grow. But finally he nodded.

"Is there anyone close to him that you know of," I said, "a friend or relative who may have contracted Phasger's, perhaps suffering now or possibly already dead from it, that might inspire Mr. Borensen to make such a generous contribution?"

Another sigh. "Frankly, no."

"Well, isn't this kind of contribution unusual?"

"It is." Something about the contribution did seem to bother him. "Mr. Hammer, there is generally paperwork we must provide to the effect that our institute is an organization funded by charity, giving the donor a tax benefit. Mr. Borensen did not pursue that avenue. My sole contact with him were these two checks."

I thought about that.

Then I asked, "Doctor, have you received any similar contributions, from donors otherwise unknown to you, over the past, say, five years?"

Impatience was tightening his face. "I don't know that I want to answer that, Mr. Hammer. I am willing to respond to you on the basis of the cancelled checks you presented me... and, frankly, I read the newspapers, and know that Mr. Borensen died a suicide recently... but I see no reason for our conversation to go further..." He rose. "Now, if you'll *excuse* me, I have rather important work to get back to."

He came around his desk and I got up and faced him, blocking the way. Not threateningly, just blocking it.

"I have important work to do, too, Doc. You're chasing a killer called Phasger's Syndrome. I'm chasing down a killer who doesn't have a name yet, but he's killed many times, and will continue doing so until I eradicate this human disease."

He studied my face. "Mr. Hammer, have you ever seen a psychiatrist?"

"Once," I said. "Didn't work out. Answer my question, Doctor— have you received similar contributions in recent years, possibly not always twenty-five thousand but certainly in that vicinity?"

"…Yes."

"Any repeat contributions from any of those donors?"

"Occasionally, as with Mr. Borensen, there have been several donations of that size. But nothing regular. And no personal contact."

"None of them wanting help claiming a fat tax deduction?"

This was something that clearly had bothered him. He said, "No, sir. Not one. Do you… do you have an idea why they might do that?"

"Yes. These people wanted to attract a minimum amount of attention. They paid their money and disappeared."

"*Paid*…?"

"Just a theory I'm working on, Doc. Would you be willing to provide a list of names and addresses for these other big donors?"

His chin came up. "Well, no. Why should you expect me to? You're just a private investigator, Mr. Hammer."

"That makes me an officer of the court."

"Be that as it may—no." He was firm. "Bring me a court order, however, and I'll provide that list."

I moved away from him, easing toward the door. "Fair enough. You'll be hearing from Patrick Chambers, Captain of Homicide, NYPD. When exactly, I can't say. But I would go ahead and get that list together. And might I make another suggestion?"

A bitter little smile formed. "I'm quite sure I can't stop you, Mr. Hammer."

"Take on some security. Twenty-four hour security."

"We have a security man who…"

"Not 'man.' *Men.* With guns and military experience. I can give you the name of a good agency out of Manhattan—I'm part of only a two-person operation and couldn't handle it for you."

He was shaking his head. "This is *incredible*… Why on earth—"

"The human disease I mentioned might consider you a loose end and come looking for you. You could get infected. It wouldn't hurt like Phasger's, Doc, but I promise you, it'll be just as fatal."

He took the name.

Newburgh was less than half an hour from Cold Spring, and by mid-afternoon I was pulling into the driveway of Valley Vista Sanitarium, right up to the unwelcoming gate.

I went through the usual protocol, and then I was in Billy's room at his bedside with Velda just across from me. The little guy looked good, eyes bright, his smile ready, though he occasionally winced ("It's these damn ribs, Mike—they got me bound up tighter than a bundle of *Sunday News* right off the truck").

I said, "Velda tells me you've identified Borensen from those crime scene photos."

He nodded emphatically. "Oh, that's the hit-and-run bastard, all right. But Velda says, Sunday night, the guy did the Dutch act. So I guess the point's, whatchacallit … moot?"

I shook my head. "No, Billy, that suicide was really a homicide."

He shrugged just a bit—probably hurt his ribs to do more. "Either way you slice it, Mike, I'm off the firin' line. You gotta get me back to my stand! That kid Duck-Duck's an okay fill-in, but over the long haul, he'll put me outa business."

I patted his shoulder. "You'll be out of here soon, Billy. But I spoke to the doc and he wants you a few more days. So hang in there."

Velda was frowning at me, just a little.

I said, "I'm going to grab a smoke. Kitten, you want to keep me company?"

Then Velda and I were again down at the end of the hall, me on a chair and her on the nearest cushion of the couch, in the company of ancient magazines but no other visitors. I plucked a Lucky out of a half-gone pack. She had her arms folded and was giving me something very near a cross look. She was in a green jumpsuit this time, looking even more like a curvy commando.

"Okay, Mike, enough's enough. I like Billy fine, but sharing a room with him for… how many days now? Sleeping in a recliner? I'm ready to break out of this joint."

I waved out a match, drew in cigarette smoke, exhaled it. "I know, doll. Real soon."

"*How* soon?"

"Like I told Billy, a couple of days."

Her frown deepened. "What's the *point*, with Borensen dead?"

"The point, baby, is somebody *made* that Viking dead."

"…Our middle-of-the-night caller?"

"Bet on it."

The frown eased off a tad. "I get that, Mike, but with Borensen out of the picture, how is Billy still a target?"

"A couple of ways. This killer is a nut, but he's also a professional. He got paid for taking Billy out, and—even after personally killing the guy who hired it—he may feel he has to carry out the contract."

She wasn't buying it. "That's crazy."

"Well, so's our killer. But more likely he views Billy as a loose end, and he's definitely tying those off. Ask Borensen—just don't expect much of an answer."

The frown was gone but her eyes were tight. "How is Billy a loose end with Borensen gone?"

"Billy can confirm that Borensen drove the hit-and-run car, and if Pat mounts an exhaustive investigation into the full picture of the late Leif, Billy would provide the motive for Borensen hiring a contract on yours truly."

She just stared at me, arms folded, the beautiful brown eyes cold. "How dumb do you think I am?"

"Not dumb at all, baby."

Her eyes were slits now and the full lips managed to set themselves in a narrow line. "It's not *Billy* you want on ice. Not at this point." She jerked a thumb at the shelf of her bosom. "It's *me*."

I held up my hands in surrender. She had me. She did have me.

I said, "I won't deny that's a factor. I'm a target for a madman, a madman who—despite being a twisted piece of shit—has been a successful professional killer for some time. You want me out there worrying about you, and getting my own head blown off?"

Her mouth turned into lush lips again, and the eyes warmed. "I know, Mike. I understand. But I'm not some helpless female. You remember me, don't you? Your partner in crime? The broad who shot down the last assassin sicced on you?"

I put the cigarette out prematurely and went over to sit by her on the couch. I slipped my arm around her, drew her close.

"Let me handle this, kitten. Please. Just for a few days. Then if I haven't brought this mess to a successful conclusion, you can come back and join in. Play Tonto to my Lone Ranger."

She smiled some, then gave me a little nod that was a big capitulation.

"You think those two slept together?" I asked her. "You know, around the campfire?"

"Shut up," she said, smiling some more. Then she asked, "What's the latest?"

I told her about my visit to the institute in nearby Cold Spring, including a thorough breakdown of the disease they were currently researching round the clock.

She shivered. "Spare me the gruesome details, Mike. Why go into that, anyway? Maybe you are the sadistic bastard some people think you are."

"Probably, and there's nobody researching a cure for that. The thing is, I think Phasger's Syndrome is the key here."

She cocked her head and an arc of dark hair swung. "In what way?"

"Understand, doll, this is a theory, and the paint on it isn't even dry."

Tiny smile. "Okay. I won't sit down on it and I won't touch anything. But what are you thinking, Mike?"

"I think," I said slowly, "that our hitman among hitmen has this very disease."

"*What?*"

I grinned at her. "I think he has Phasger's Syndrome, and the clock has been ticking, and right now it's ticking louder and louder, and the calendar pages of his existence are flying off faster and faster, like in an old movie."

"Why do you think that?"

"Leif Borensen, who had no personal connection to the disease, wrote two checks for twenty-five thousand bucks to that institute."

A thoughtful frown. "Why?"

"Because he was paying off two murder-for-hire contracts with our middle-of-the-night caller."

Her eyes showed white all around now. "You mean… the pro killer Borensen hired insisted on payment by way of contributions to that research institute?"

"You got it, honey. And I think for some time now, months certainly, possibly years, this very successful hitman has channeled everything he earns into that institute, hoping against hope for a cure. The checks go directly to Dr. Beech's facility."

Now the lovely eyes were narrow. "Two checks from Borensen of twenty-five grand each. Two contracts? First, the faked suicide of Martin Foster, and second…"

"Wiping out a guy named Hammer," I said.

She thought about it. "And you figure, if you can get the institute's records, we'll find more high-ticket checks from other clients of the killer's."

"Exactly right, doll. That will be a job for Pat and his troops, though. But a whole lot of open homicides are going to get cleared up, and the slobs who hired them done will get rounded up and face life without parole or better still get a ride on Old Sparky."

She shook her head, as if trying to get the absurdity and the enormity of it all to gel. "How does this lunatic calling you and challenging you to a duel of sorts figure into this?"

"Don't you see it, Velda? It figures *right* in. He's dying. I'm guessing in a matter of weeks, the serious Phasger's stuff starts kicking in. Well, before that ignoble ending, he wants to go out on a high goddamn note. He sees me as the only other killer around worthy of that honor."

"If you're right," she said, "maybe… maybe he *wants* you to kill him."

"If so," I said, "he came to the right place."

Before I left Valley Vista, I stopped by Billy's bedside again, with Velda opposite me once more.

"Bill buddy," I said, "is there anything you can think of, however small, that might be of help? Maybe something you mentioned to the police and they didn't seem excited, so you forgot about it?"

The wrinkled face wrinkled further. "You know, there *is* something. Not something I ever told the cops, 'cause I didn't know what it had to do with the price of beans. But there was this girl, this kind of… hippie chick. Glasses, short black hair, nice build, though."

Velda smirked at me. "Sounds like your kind of lead."

I ignored that. "What about this hippie chick?"

"She came around to the newsstand, a day or two after the hit-and-run. She wanted to know anything at all about how this

Blazen guy died. How the damn thing happened. I asked her why I should tell her anything—I mean, she was nobody to me."

"And?"

"She said she'd been working with Blazen. Sort of his legman and, you know, researcher, helping on the writing. She does freelance for that giveaway rag, the leftie thing… what is it?"

"*The Village Voice?*" Velda asked.

"That's it. She was sad. She'd been crying. You could tell she really liked the old boy. A week later, she come back with a bunch of questions written down, but I didn't have any more for her than I did the other time."

I leaned in. "She ever give you a name, Billy?"

"Yeah. She did. Marcy. Never got a last name, or if so, I forgot the damn thing. But she, you know, looked like a Marcy, so I remembered it. Does that help, Mike?"

"It just might," I said.

CHAPTER TWELVE

The state of mind that was Greenwich Village was changing, beatnik black giving way to rainbow tie-dye, finger-snapping egocentric poetry getting drowned out by clap-along protest folk songs. Other things stayed the same, like the zigzag streets, art-gallery sidewalks, espresso joints, intimate jazz clubs, and theater ranging from Circle in the Square respectability to strip-joint sleaze.

There was also no shortage of bookshops, running mostly to secondhand, and that's where I asked about a girl called Marcy with short black hair and glasses, who might be doing research on the history of show business in the city. I got nowhere on this sunny but cool afternoon until I tried the Paper Book Gallery on the corner of Sullivan and West Third, a Beat Generation landmark still advertising poetry readings even though the kid at the register had long hippie hair and little square-lensed glasses.

"You might mean Marcy Bloom," the kid said. He wore a black vest over a paisley shirt. "That sounds like the project she's been working on. I delivered her some old magazines she ordered, like a couple of weeks ago."

"Then you know where she lives," I said. Not a question.

He frowned. "I can't give out a customer's address, if that's what you're after. Would you want me giving out *your* address, mister?"

I dug out my wallet and he was shaking his head.

"Save your bread, man. I'm no sell-out."

But he *was* a weed smoker, judging by his dreamy eyes and the pungent scent clinging to his clothes.

I flipped the wallet open and shut, just long enough for him to glimpse the badge there. That it went with my P.I. ticket and not a job on the PD was a distinction I didn't figure he would make.

He had to look it up in a card file, but he got me the address. He was shaking and afraid.

"She's not in any trouble, son," I told him, taking the scribbled-on slip of paper he handed me. "And neither are you. Appreciate the help."

He nodded and started working up his story for his pals about how he'd been hassled by the man.

Marcy Bloom's building was a white-washed brick three-story that looked like a strong wind might crumble it. Green shutters and black ironwork dressed it up, and some of the city's few remaining gas lamps lent a certain charm. But I wondered how long the quaint buildings on these cobblestone side streets could stand up against the intrusion of the world of commerce.

On the second floor landing, I knocked at 2B. As I waited, the door across the way opened, and I turned. In the half-opened doorway, a skinny guy with a shoulder-length pile of curly brown hair was giving me a what-the-hell-are-you-doing-here look. In his mid-twenties or so, he wore a faded maroon T-shirt with a cracked white peace symbol, and his jeans looked older than he did.

I gave him a smile that wasn't pleasant. "Something I can do for you, man?"

He retreated and shut the door, hard.

I shrugged to nobody, turned back and knocked again on the paint-blistered door. I was just getting ready to knock a third time when a girl answered so suddenly I almost jumped back.

"Sorry," she said chirpily, as if we were old friends, "I had to throw something on."

She was petite but curvy, with boyishly short dark hair and big dark blue eyes that the black-framed, big-lensed glasses perched on her pert nose could hardly contain. She had a brightness and energy about her that came across right now, and was at least as cute as her navy white-polka-dotted mini-dress. She was maybe twenty-three and made me wish I was.

"Say," she said. "You're Mike Hammer!"

Surprised to be recognized, particularly by someone her age, I admitted it nonetheless. Was she Marcy Bloom? She was. She seemed not at all surprised I'd come calling.

Looking past me, her cuteness took on sharp edges, and she said, "*Shack!* Quit that! Be good!"

I glanced behind me just in time to see that door across the way slam again.

"Don't mind Shack," she said, her smile dimpling one side of the adorable face. "He's harmless. Poor puppy dog's just in love with me."

"But is he house-broken?"

She smiled at that and took me by the elbow like I was her

father giving her away at a wedding. She ushered me not down the aisle but into her apartment.

"You saved me a trip," she said.

"How did I do that?"

She asked for my hat and coat, which she promptly dropped onto a chair. Then she led me past an odd work area on a braided throw rug in the center of the living room, with a table whose legs had been sawed off to put it a foot-and-a-half off the floor, a typewriter on it, and a throw pillow for a chair. The table had stacks of manuscript paper and various research materials, books, magazines, notebooks, all in cheerful disarray.

My hostess deposited me on a threadbare couch while she sat on the floor like an Indian, giving me a glimpse of white inner thighs and dark panties. Well, more than a glimpse.

She looked up at me like I was a guru and she was ready to learn the meaning of life. The way she was sitting, I could have told her.

"I've been trying to get the nerve up," she said, "to come see you at your office."

The couch, like the other furnishings in the Early Salvation Army decor, sat well out from the wall, which like the others was consumed by bookcases. Some were homemade concrete-block affairs, plus thrift-shop shelving she'd scrounged. She had built an enviable library, no doubt as secondhand as the furniture, the fiction running from *Pride and Prejudice* to *Peyton Place*, the non-fiction heavy on journalism and film and theater criticism.

She said, "What brings you around to see me, Mr. Hammer?"

"Maybe we should start," I replied, "with why *you* were thinking of coming to see *me*?"

Hands on her bare knees, she rocked back and forth a little on her crossed legs. As the original Billy Batson said, *Holy moly.*

"Okay, I'll start," she said. The big eyes grew bigger. "I've been following this crazy thing in the papers and on TV. Do you know, when your name first turned up, I'd never *heard* of you? I'm from Ohio, which is my excuse. But from snippets in the newspaper stories, I got the picture—you're a real *character.*"

"I get that sometimes," I admitted.

She smiled and rocked. "So I did some research on you. Mostly at the library, but also some old magazines at a bookstore I frequent."

"The Paper Book Galley," I said.

Her eyes got wide again, like I'd pulled a rabbit out of a hat. Or somewhere. "You *are* a detective!"

"That's the rumor. So you researched me. What did that tell you?"

"That some of what the papers have been saying is b.s.—like the supposed robbery attempt at your office, and how the police were looking into that cabbie's life to see why someone would want to take it, and how that high-society bridal shower got interrupted by an armed robber. And, of course, how you just *happened* to be there for all three. Killing the first two bad guys, and your secretary taking down the third."

"You left out the newsstand shooting."

She nodded, out of rhythm with her rocking. "I was saving that for last, because that was what made me start really, seriously thinking about approaching you directly. Did you know I spoke to Billy, that little person who runs the newsstand, several times?"

I nodded back. "I did know. He told me you had, which is why and how I tracked you down."

"So then you know I was Richard Blazen's legman?"

"Yeah." I gave all that exposed skin an unabashed look. "Coincidentally, I'm a leg man myself."

That only made her laugh. I'd thought maybe it would embarrass her into covering up a little. I've always been big on decorum.

"When I was running through that list of fatalities," she said, "I left the most recent one out. The most significant one."

"Leif Borensen," I said.

She nodded. "Was that *really* suicide, like the papers say?"

"No."

"Didn't think so. But it confuses me. I figured he was the party responsible for all this mayhem. He ran down Mr. Blazen in a car, and tried to have you killed several times before going after the little newsstand fella. Am I right?"

I answered with my own question: "Why do you figure Borensen was responsible for the attempts on my life?"

She shrugged. "I told you I researched you. I'm a *ferocious* researcher, Mike. I'll call you 'Mike' and you call me 'Marcy.' Kind of a nice ring to it, Mike and Marcy. Anyway, you're known to go on the hunt for anybody who hurts or... or especially *kills*... your friends. You're famous for it."

"That's 'infamous,'" I said.

Her smile was barely there. "That would depend on whether someone thought you were a bad person. I mean by that, someone who thinks it's wrong of you to go out and, well, try to get even."

"I don't just try, Marcy."

Her eyebrows went up and down. "I know. And I may live in Greenwich Village and write articles for the *Voice*, but I am an old-fashioned Midwestern girl at heart. I *like* to see scores settled. So, me? I think you're a good person."

She seemed at once ten years old and forty-five.

"Nice to know, Marcy." I leaned forward and said, "You say you were Blazen's 'legman,' but really you were a lot more than that… right? I figure *you* were the one doing the writing. An old PR guy may know how to put together a press release, but not a whole book."

She was nodding, rocking a little while I talked, stopping when she talked.

"You're right, Mike. Richard Blazen knew everybody in local theater, going back to the 1930s, and in TV production back to the late '40s. He had stories like you couldn't imagine—the back-stabbing by much admired stars, who was gay and who wasn't, producers screwing over their backers, producers screwing over their *stars*, the sleeping around by just about everybody, the gangsters who backed productions to give their mistresses roles in shows, and drugs, drugs, drugs. Some of the show biz types who are so critical of my pot-smoking generation were outrageous hypocrites, snorting coke and shooting up H. Mr. Blazen knew it all." She grinned and rocked again. "It's going to be a fabulous book."

That stopped me for a moment. "You're going on with the project?"

"Oh yes. I have all the material here. It's still a big job. I have to fact-check, when the people he talks about are still alive. It's a legal thing."

"You say 'talks' like he's still around."

"That's how it feels sometimes. See, here's how we went about it—I'd interview him on a tape recorder, and then we'd have the tapes transcribed. I have pages and pages of the stuff."

"So it really is a big job."

"Enormous! But it'll *make* me. Put me on the map, as the cliché goes." Gently, she pointed a finger at me. "The reason I wanted to see you, Mike, was to find out what you knew about this awful Borensen person. To see if you'd go on the record that he was the one who ran down Mr. Blazen."

"I can do that." I sat forward, springs in the couch cushion whining under my tail. "But first I want to know what *you* know, Marcy... about your Mr. Blazen and Leif Borensen."

"You bet." She bounded up and sat next to me on the couch, with a leg tucked under her, giving me a new angle on how artistically black silk panties could contrast with white creamy thighs.

Hammer, a voice said, *she's young enough to be your daughter.*

Another voice said, *But she* isn't *your daughter.*

"Mr. Blazen knew Martin Foster for a very long time," Marcy said. "Did PR work for him in the early days, and off-and-on in later years, too... and *always* respected and admired the man. Mr. Blazen said Martin Foster was a rare class act in an often no-class business."

"I knew Foster a little," I said. "I'd agree."

She continued: "So when it became known that Martin Foster was planning to bring this Leif Borensen in as his co-producer, Mr. Blazen went to see his old friend, and warned him that this Hollywood pretender was no one to get involved with. That the man had been in league with mobsters since his unsuccessful stint as an actor."

"Borensen was *still* mobbed up," I said. "Right to the end. He's been a major West Coast money laundry for the boys for decades."

"Yes, Mr. Blazen knew that, too, or at least had come to that conclusion. And he was appalled to find out that Borensen was dating Foster's daughter, Gwen."

"Worming his way in," I said.

She leaned forward, the cute face painfully earnest. "But, Mr. Hammer, isn't this sorry, sordid affair now at an end? After the suicide of Leif Borensen? Only you say it was *not* suicide. Which makes it murder."

"It's murder, all right."

"*You* didn't do it, did you?"

The casualness of that caught me off guard.

I said, "Hell, no. Marcy, consider the three attempts on my life. You said it yourself—Borensen tried to *have* me killed. He didn't have the balls to try to do it himself."

And I told her that the bastard had been dealing with a top-dollar contract killer, with a stable of hitmen, and was now tying off loose ends. Including Leif himself.

"So this big-league professional assassin," she said, "is who you're looking for."

"Yes. Would you like to help?"

"Just tell me how."

I put a hand on her shoulder. "What I need from you is a specific piece of information that might well lead me to this killer."

"If I have that information, it's yours. But what exactly do you need to know?"

I leaned back and a couch spring played stick-'em-up in my spine. "Maybe you're still too much of an Ohio girl to know, Marcy, but there are five major crime families in New York. I am assuming Leif Borensen was aligned with one of them, going back to his drug-peddling days."

"You think he's been in with the same mob all these years?"

"Very likely. Those kind of people get their hooks in, and they stay in. Now, I'm known to all of these families, and they're known to me. If you... or rather the late Richard Blazen... can point me to the right crime family, I may be able to ascertain the name of this contract killer."

She nodded slowly. "That does make sense. They're who Leif Borensen would have gone to, to obtain a professional killer."

I grinned at her. "You're right on the beam, kid."

The earnest look returned, with some confusion mixed in. "You're thinking maybe I know a name, or the name of the Mafia family... but I don't, really."

"It should have come up in research, and in the taped interviews."

She shook her head, frustrated. "Well, I'm sure that name *is* something I saw or heard out of Mr. Blazen. But it wouldn't mean anything to me. I have a vague memory that some Italian names came up in this context, which is probably no surprise."

"No, no surprise. But the name of the crime family, or a member of it, would almost have to be in your notes or those transcripts, right?"

"Right." She rose. An air of determination accompanied her. "We have a big job in front of us, Mike. Maybe you'd like some coffee?"

"I would. Milk and sugar."

I thought she was going to go off to a kitchenette and make some, but she went to her door, opened it and crossed to knock at her horny neighbor's.

The kid answered, more hangdog than puppy dog, as if maybe she was going to paddle him with a rolled-up paper.

"Shack, would you be a dear and run down and get us some coffee at the deli? Maybe some sandwiches." She called across to me. "Sandwich, Mike?"

"Sure! Corned beef and Swiss, cold, plenty of hot mustard."

She told him, "I'll have the usual."

"Bacon, lettuce, tomato, mayo?" he asked.

"*Hold* the mayo," she said, almost testily. "That's the usual. You need money?"

"No. You can pay me later."

"Get yourself something, too. I'm going to have you join us, if you're not doing anything."

That brightened him. "Yeah? Sure, I'm available. You need help, Marcy?"

She was still in her doorway, he in his.

"We're going to be sorting through some of the interview transcripts," she said. "We can use your sharp eyes. You up for that, sweetie?"

"You bet!"

"Great. But before you go down to the deli, could you come over and carry the manuscript boxes in from my bedroom?"

"Glad to!"

From the sound of his voice, I could tell her bedroom was a

place he would very much like to visit.

She came bouncing back to me, her full breasts making the white dots on the dark mini-dress dance. When Good Neighbor Shack was back in his own apartment, that bedroom was somewhere I would very much like to visit myself.

Don't do this to Velda, a voice said.

Velda who? another voice said.

When Shack came in with three storage-file boxes stacked in his arms, and then plopped them down on the floor near Marcy's low-lying work station, I said to her, "Brother. You weren't kidding."

"He was a talker," she said, "my Mr. Blazen."

Shack trotted off toward the bedroom again, and I asked her, "There's more?"

"There's more. Maybe you should help him."

Nine boxes in all.

Not all of it was transcripts, but each box had its share. Included were newspaper clippings and photo files, plus Blazen's early attempts in longhand at writing the book himself, before wising up that he needed a ghost.

After Shack got back with the deli food, which we ate as we worked, he sat on the couch next to me—well, putting a cushion between us, which became a shared desk. Marcy returned to the floor and her chopped-off table. She continued to sit cross-legged, angled toward us, and at one point Shack and I caught ourselves both looking at the same time. We just rolled our eyes at each other, forming a bond in our mutual lechery.

The three of us couldn't read all that stuff, not in detail. Transcript is hard to read anyway, with its lack of paragraphs and occasional misrecorded words and phrases. The idea was to skim and scan and try to catch any mention of Borensen and his mob ties, as well as any Italian name that might turn up.

Finally, almost three hours in, Marcy blurted in mock-*My Fair Lady* fashion, "By George, I think I've got it!… Do you know a gangster called Joey Pep, Mike?"

"Joey Pepitone," I said, frowning. A longtime *capo* in the Bonetti mob family. "I know him, all right."

"Could he be our man?"

I was nodding. "He could. He sure could. And I can check that out right away. Shack, much appreciated. Marcy, you have a phone?"

She did, in her bedroom—which was a mattress on the floor surrounded by more walls of books—and I used it and her Manhattan phonebook.

A maid or anyway somebody on the household staff answered, and I gave my name and asked for Gwen.

"Mike, it's nice to hear your voice."

But I wasn't sure it really was. We'd been ships who passed in the night, and maybe I shouldn't be pulling back into port.

"Honey, did you ever see Leif mingling or talking with anybody who struck you as… disreputable? Any associate who struck you as shady? I know that's vague, but—"

"Actually, yes," she said quickly. "I was going to call and say something to you, Mike, because I've been thinking, going over so much in my mind, so many things. I don't know the man's name, but there was a slick, nasty-looking character who Leif would treat with… well, undue respect."

"Did he ever drop by your apartment, this guy?"

"Not that I know of. But if Leif and I were at 21 or the Stork, this well-dressed creepy character might turn up in a booth with one or two flashy women. Leif would excuse himself, and go talk to him, just briefly. Like he was… paying his respects. Is *that* anything, Mike?"

"Are you doing anything tonight?"

My shift of gears threw her a little. "Not really. I've had a tough day. Among other things, I made arrangements to ship Leif's body back to Hollywood. Let *them* bury the bum."

That made me grin, but of course I have a sick sense of humor. "What would you say if I asked you to go out dancing with me?"

"Well… what?"

"Sounds a little inappropriate, or at least it might look that way. But I have a real good reason. I want to give you a chance to identify that 'creepy character.'"

I filled her in and said I'd come by in a cab and pick her up in half an hour or so.

When I returned to the living room, Marcy was walking Shack out, her arm in his as it had been in mine earlier. "Thank you, Shack. You're such a dear. Such a wonderful friend."

His hangdog puss got longer. "Oh, Marcy. No guy wants to hear that. The friend bit."

"Now, you know that's how it has to be."

He was stumbling out toward 2B, as if the few steps were a thousand miles, when she shut her door.

"You're pretty rough on the kid," I said, reaching for my hat and raincoat on the chair where she'd tossed them.

"Oh, Shack should know better. Are you leaving, Mike?"

"I am. Here's my card. I've written my home phone on it, too. Anything occurs to you, any hour of the day or night, let me know."

"Well, you're welcome here any time, Mike."

My God, what an invitation. A stunning little Love Child was ready to corrupt an old rake.

Just as I was going, I said, "What do you mean, Shack should know better?"

"Well, Mike," she said, with a big beautiful smile. "I *am* a lesbian, after all."

CHAPTER THIRTEEN

Not so long ago, when you got within a few blocks of the place, a riot might have been going on, judging by the backed-up traffic, night-piercing floodlights and crowd noise spilling down the skyscraper canyon. You'd have to hoof it the rest of the way because even if your car or cab got through, a police barricade would be waiting, and mounted cops would be herding an excited throng of kids who looked like refugees from *American Bandstand* mixed with swells in gowns and tuxes, swarming the sidewalk all the way to Broadway at least. Only a few limos conveying celebrities to the hottest night spot in town got squeezed through the sawhorses, because a whisper of fame and money could out-yell any crowd.

But four years later, on a week night, the Peppermint Lounge on West Forty-fifth didn't even have a doorman when the cab dropped Gwen and me off. A few patrons, couples mostly, were coming in and out, in no hurry, and lackluster rock 'n' roll bled out, blaring when a door opened, muffling when it closed.

"My," Gwen said, on my arm. "What a difference from the last time I was here!"

Her blonde hair ponytailed back, she wore a white mini-dress, matching go-go boots, and a knee-length camel coat with a white mink collar. I let my porkpie hat and trenchcoat make my fashion statement.

I said, "When was that?"

"Oh, '61, '62."

Now the place was a shadow of its former faddish self. The candy-striped canopy drooped under red letters spelling out the club's name on a cracked white facade. A window display of photos of yesterday's celebrities reminded today's visitors that the joint was "World Famous"—and of course when you have to post reminders, you aren't world famous any more.

We checked our coats and moved through the bar into the shabby L-shaped club, met by a short, hawk-faced maître d', who seemed depressed he wasn't getting the big tips any more. He showed us to a table up front in the sparsely lighted, low-ceilinged, under-populated showroom, though mirrors surrounding the elevated dance floor were doing their best to make it seem bigger. A four-piece combo on stage was dragging its ass through "The Peppermint Twist." Only half a dozen dancers were out there, college kids doing the Watusi and adult tourists feeling obligated to do the dance the house helped popularize.

In their white tops and red ski pants, all the waitresses were cute, since they doubled as on-stage dancers, and our redheaded one was no exception. She had to work at being bubbly, though. She wouldn't make enough tips tonight to cover carfare.

Looking around at the half-filled place, Gwen said, "The last time I was here, you know who was on that dance floor? Greta Garbo!"

"She should have come tonight," I said, "if she wanted to be alone."

"It *does* seem more a museum exhibit than a nightclub," she said, with something of a shudder. Then she beamed at me, clutched my hand. "Mike, it was nice to hear from you. As you can imagine, it's been a real drag since, well, since that son-of-a-bitch fiancé of mine got himself killed."

Appeared she was doing well getting over Borensen's passing. Not all mourners could carry off white like she did.

"You may not give a damn who killed Leif," I said. "I mean, after all—somebody did you a kind of favor. But keep in mind— the same somebody killed your father."

"*Leif* killed my father."

"*Had* him killed." I squeezed her hand. "I asked you out tonight, honey, not to cheer you up but to see if you can identify that creep you saw your late unlamented Leif sucking up to."

"The *creep's* the one who…?"

"No. But he can lead me to the assassin. If this place were busier, it wouldn't be so tricky. But when our drinks come, take a sip and glance around like you're taking in the whole place… but glom the guy sitting in back at a table in the corner, on your side."

"It's awfully dark, Mike."

The ceiling spotlights aimed at the stage were about it for illumination.

"I know," I said, "but do your best. Tell me if there's at least a possibility it's the creep in question."

The waitress brought my Four Roses and ginger, and Gwen's peppermint schnapps. When I handed the redhead a twenty and said keep the change, I made a friend for life, or at least the rest of the evening. Meanwhile, Gwen sipped the sweet liqueur and glanced casually around.

She didn't say anything till the band was between numbers. With a sweet feminine smile that might have accompanied almost anything, she leaned in to say something that it didn't.

"Mike, that's *definitely* the scumball whose ass Leif used to kiss."

I sipped my highball and smiled back at her. "I'm going to go back there and just say hello. Listen, if things should get lively, just sit tight. Like the man said, I will return… unless I get killed or something."

Her facial expression stayed casual and even amused, but her hand gripping my sleeve wasn't. "Mike, you're *scaring* me."

"Not a bad thing to be, considering."

Because this was a no-cover-charge joint, the path to the bar was kept clear. When I was almost there, I veered off the central aisle and wove through the tight-packed but mostly empty tables and chairs, coming to a stop at the table for four where one man sat. Where he always sat.

Small but compactly muscular, Joey Pepitone wore a dark gray sharkskin suit with white silk shirt and black silk tie. Diamonds winked off tie-pin and cufflinks, and gold rings winked back from slender fingers that had never seen a real day's work. He was a slimily handsome hoodlum whose most distinctive features were his sleepy eyes, constant faint sneer, heavy dark eyebrows and prematurely gray hair. He'd be a living, breathing cliché, if he and his ilk weren't where the cliché came from.

"Mike Hammer," he said looking up at me. His voice was a

smooth tenor. "I never took you for a rock 'n' roll fan."

I pulled out a chair and sat across from him, leaning back with my arms folded. "Nah, I'm more a classical guy. Give me the old masters. And I don't mean Joey Dee and the Starliters."

He smiled, just a little. He had an iceless tumbler of dark liquid in front of him and a cigarette going, waiting in an ashtray for his attention.

"Pretty girl you got with you tonight," he said off-handedly, nodding toward Gwen at our table up front. He had a decent look at her in profile, since her chair was angled toward the stage.

"Would you believe it? She's grieving over her fiancé's death. Kind of an almost widow."

He pretended that didn't mean anything to him. "Well, I hope she's wearing black undies. Otherwise, she seems a little disrespectful."

I let that pass. "Business always this shitty, Joe? Nothing like being yesterday's big thing, huh?"

"We do all right on the weekends," he said. "And the tourists keep us going in between."

The success of the Peppermint Lounge had been a fluke. It had been a gay bar Joey Pep took over from a pal of his who had to lam it out of town. Once he took over the joint, Joey worked out of the back room, where he gave the Bonetti family's blessing (for a piece of the action) to various illegal activities—loan-sharking, fencing, bookmaking.

Then the hot band he hired, just for show, started pulling in the kids, and the Twist craze took off, and suddenly a mob front was a legitimate goldmine. But right now, that goldmine seemed tapped out.

"Did you come here to depress me, Hammer, or do you just like to watch young stuff shake it on a dance floor?"

I grinned at him. "I can do both at the same time, Joey. I can include chewing bubble gum if you like."

He smiled back, but of course the sneer was in it. "Well, thanks for stopping by, Hammer. Always good to renew an acquaintance. You need a cab? I'll have one called for you."

"Joey, I just got here. I'm trying to show the little lady a good time."

"Is that what you're doing." He picked up the cigarette, drew in smoke, then sent it my way. "Blow, why don't you? You're very old news."

I looked around us. "Then I'd seem to be in the right place. Why don't we keep it friendly, Joey? I just stopped by to see how you're doing, after your tragic loss."

"What tragic loss would that be?"

I nodded toward Gwen, sipping her schnapps. "The loss of a longtime, valued business associate."

"Maybe you know what you're talking about, Hammer, but I don't."

I uncrossed my arms and met his sneer with my own. "Don't be coy, Joey—Leif Borensen goes way back with the Bonettis, and I hear you were his contact man. He was a kind of one-man Peppermint Lounge himself, wasn't he? A guy who could provide a front and be a cash laundry when needed, and other times a cash cow, pulling down some real Hollywood bucks."

He looked past me and nodded. I glanced back and saw two big men in skinny ties coming my way. Their dark suits looked sewn on. But their bulges seemed to be muscle and some occasional fat, so at least they weren't packing.

"Lenny, Turk," he said to them.

One was on either side of me. They were tall and they were wide, and the fists hanging at their side were like hams.

Pepitone looked up and gave them the sneer-smile. "You remember Mike Hammer, don't you, fellas? He used to be a big deal, a long, long time ago." He lowered his eyes to meet mine and gave me the same nasty smile. "Lenny and Turk here, they were big deals, too, *not* so long ago. Pro wrestlers. All my bouncers are ex-wrestlers, Hammer. One look at them and most smart-asses piss themselves."

"I don't have to go," I said.

"Oh yes you do… Put Mr. Hammer in a cab."

A big hand latched onto my left elbow, and another one latched onto my right.

"Don't worry about Miss Foster," Pepitone said as I was hauled up and out of the chair. "I'll see she gets home safely."

Right now she was on the dance floor with a college kid, doing the frug. She didn't notice the bum's rush I was getting, and that was all right. I wanted her kept out of it.

The boys lifted me up and walked me, if walked is the right word when your feet aren't touching the ground, through the tables and chairs and out into the bar and through the front door, where we paused under the canopy. Turk, shaved bald with dark eyebrows on a shelf of forehead, a handlebar mustache over thick lips, slipped behind me, took both my arms and yanked my elbows behind my back, making the upper half of me lean forward, while

Beatle-haired Lenny, with beady black eyes crowding what must once have been a nose, lumbered to the curb to flag a cab that was a good half-block down.

Lenny was doing that when I rammed my head up under Turk's chin and as his neck snapped back and his grip loosened on my arms, I pulled away and swung around behind him and kicked him with the flat of a gum-soled foot behind the knee, one of the few places he wasn't muscle-bound. Turk went down on the other knee, like he was waiting for a king to knight him, but I crowned him instead, with two fists coming down like sledges on the back of his bald skull. He belly-flopped onto the cement, by which time Lenny, wide-eyed, wild-eyed, was charging at me like a bull. When he was almost on me, I swung my leg around and let his ugly face taste the gum sole. He staggered back, spitting teeth like bloody Chiclets, and then I shoved my left forearm into what little neck he had and he started coughing and gargling the foamy blood in his mouth. To one side, Turk was getting up, and I grabbed onto him by the tie and a fistful of too-tight suit and flung him into Lenny, sending them both down in a pile. I let them wrestle for a few seconds, catching my breath, then went over and started kicking the shit out of them. Muscles or not, they had ribs and they hadn't been in the ring for a while, so their stomachs had some flab going, and I kicked them there, too, just till they puked all over each other. Somehow they managed to get to their feet, so I got out the .45 and let them see where bullets blossom. That froze them, and I slapped them with the side of the barrel, in one swift hard continuous move, like Moe slapping Larry and Curly in one hilarious swing, only seeing those guys tumble to the cement unconscious was a hell of a lot funnier.

The cab had pulled up by now, and the cabbie was looking out at the two fallen, bleeding, vomit-spattered human wrecks like he was having an hallucination. He was a mick who'd been around, probably in his fifties, and looked like he was about to take off, when I waved at him with the .45, not meaning to threaten him exactly. The gun just happened to be there.

"Give me a hand with these clowns," I said.

Leaving the cab running, he came around and helped me lug the two bouncers, one at a time, into his backseat. It was like hauling beef carcasses at a slaughter house. They filled that back nicely, sprawled on top of each other like teenagers at Lover's Lane.

The cabbie was breathing hard. "God, they smell."

"Well, they're covered in puke."

"What do you want me to do with them?"

I got in my pocket and fished out some dough. "What do you think? Take 'em to the nearest emergency room."

He had the expression of a guy who couldn't decide whether to shit or go blind, but when I gave him the fifty, he saw that just fine.

As he rolled off, I smoothed myself out—neither one of the slobs had laid a glove on me—and then I went back inside the lounge and wove through the tables and chairs over to Joey Pep's table. He was goggling at me with his tongue showing, like I was a naked babe in a window.

I sat down. "Where were we?"

A guy like Joey Pep has seen a lot of things. Such people don't impress easily at all. But right now he seemed to be.

"Damnit, Hammer—where are Turk and Lenny?"

"On their way to the hospital. That cab came in handy."

He didn't know what to say. His hands were shaking and the cigarette had fallen out of his mouth onto the floor.

I patted his shoulder and grinned in his face. "Joey, ease up. Don't you know those wrestlers need a script to pull anything off? Me, I like to improvise."

"What… what kind of shape are they in?"

"Serious but stable, I'd say." I shifted in my chair. "Joey, here's the thing. Don't go hiring ex-wrestlers. Get guys who are wrestling *now*, and haven't gone to fat yet."

The redheaded waitress came over to see if we needed anything. I asked for another Four Roses and ginger, and Pepitone another bourbon.

"So, anyway, Leif Borensen," I said, sitting back.

He was lighting up a cigarette, hands steadier but not entirely recovered. "Yeah, he was ours, for a long time. What about it?"

"Had Leif broken loose from you boys, to pursue his Broadway producer ambition? Was he going straight, I mean?"

The little mobster shook his head, sighing smoke. "No, that was strictly an ego deal. But he was staying in the movie business, maybe expanding if he got a Broadway hit he could get a film out of. Come on, Hammer, you know we don't let people out till they hit retirement age."

Retirement age tended to be however old you were when you wound up in the trunk of a stolen car with your throat slashed and your nuts in your mouth. Gold watch not included.

I said, "So Borensen was still your guy?"

"Still our guy."

"Which is why he came to you, a few months ago, to get put in touch with a professional who could remove a problem he had. A problem called Martin Foster. His prospective father-in-law, no less."

Pepitone took smoke in and let it out. Quietly he said, "When you're in business with somebody, you do them favors. We had nothing against Foster and had nothing to do with his removal, either. Sometimes these business associates ask for a... referral. You know, like a doctor."

"And Borensen wanted a specialist."

He nodded, once. "He wanted a specialist."

"This is somebody you've used."

"I don't see that that's pertinent to your line of inquiry."

"Maybe not."

The redhead brought our drinks. I sipped mine. Pepitone sipped his.

I asked, "If Borensen had access to a 'specialist,' why did he pull that hit-and-run kill himself?"

He laughed and smoke came out of his nose, like a dragon. "For a stupid reason. A very stupid damn reason."

"Which was?"

He sighed. No smoke this time. "The specialist I refer to is very expensive. You don't go to a specialist for just *any* operation, right? When it's something really serious, you go to the best. And the best is who I sent Borensen to. And that was pricey."

"Twenty-five grand."

That I knew this surprised him, and his nostrils flared, like a horse rearing. "You *do* get around, Hammer. You've always had a goddamn nose. Yes. You have the figure exactly right."

I sat forward. "Are you saying Borensen ran down Dick Blazen himself because he was too *cheap* to have it done?"

He gave me a one-shoulder shrug. "Draw your own conclusions. Certainly he could have afforded another twenty-five. But some of the richest people on the planet are the tightest damn wads around. After the fact, I told him so. Said when you're dealing in matters like this, you can't treat it like one of your goddamn B-movies where you pinch every goddamn penny." He shrugged. "Of course, our friend learned his lesson, when he came to the rather obvious conclusion that running some prick down can leave witnesses."

"You mean, when he decided to have me killed, he gave up do-it-yourself, and went back to the specialist, and paid the freight."

He gave me a slow-motion shrug. "I wouldn't know, Hammer. I wasn't part of it. I just made the original referral."

I grinned at him. "You must be wishing you hadn't, about now. Because your specialist is getting way out of hand, Joey. He killed Borensen and—what you may not know since it was withheld from the papers—he staged it as a suicide that exactly mirrored the Foster one, right down to the specific type of rod."

"*What?* Why the hell would he do that?"

"Because your specialist has a screw loose. He wanted to tell me and the cops to go screw ourselves. He wanted to have a big old belly laugh on us."

He reached for the glass of bourbon and finished it.

Then he said: "To be honest with you, Hammer... we decided to drop our... specialist... when we saw that he was going after you, in such a reckless, foolhardy manner. Sending second-raters to take you on, instead of tending to business himself. No, we're done with him."

"Would you like to know why he did that?"

"Why, do you?"

"Oh yeah."

I told the Bonetti *capo* about the late-night phone call, and the killer's desire to challenge me, to take me on. To see which of us was the real killer among killers.

"He's gone off the deep end," Pepitone said, shaking his head. "Son of a bitch is screwier than an outhouse rat."

"Doesn't that worry you, Joey? This loose cannon knows where the bodies are buried, because he buried them... *for you*."

Pepitone waved that off with a gold-ring-laden hand. "Oh, he won't talk. That's not a problem. Anyway, he'll be out of the picture soon."

"Because you're removing his ass from Planet Earth?"

His smile was sly. "No. Something's doing it for us."

Not somebody—*something*.

I lighted up a smoke and smiled around it, as I got it going. "You wouldn't be referring to Phasger's Syndrome, would you?"

He grunted a laugh. "Damnit, Hammer. You have a nose. You do have a nose. Where... how... did you...? Hell with it. I don't care. As I get it, the specialist's maybe two weeks away from that disease kicking in and blotting him out, nice and slow. He thinks *he's* a killer? That shit has it all over him."

"He wants to shoot it out with me first."

"Some advice, Hammer? Don't do it. Don't go looking for him.

If you kill him, you'll be doing him a favor. Wouldn't you rather have the bastard suffer? *I* would."

"So if I asked you for his name, or his address, you wouldn't give it?"

"You'd have to haul me off and beat it out of me. And you could do that. We both know you could. But then you'd have a real problem, bigger than this asshole. You'd have to take on the Bonetti family, all their soldiers, all their guns. Is it worth it, just to have the pleasure of shooting this killer in the guts? You need to weigh the thing in your mind, Hammer. A sadistic prick like you should *want* to let that foul disease have him."

He had a point.

"Or maybe he'll track you down," he said with a shrug. "If so, maybe you'll kill his ass."

"Or he'll kill mine."

He sneer-grinned, blew out smoke. "Either way, it's a winner from where I'm sitting... Stay as long as you like, Hammer. Run a tab on the house. Take that pretty girl out on the dance floor. I'll have those long-haired dipshits play a slow tune, so an old warrior like you can keep up."

CHAPTER FOURTEEN

Indian summer had been replaced by a damp chill under a sky gone as gray as wet newspaper. A squad car was parked in the cobblestone street, half on the sidewalk, but still leaving barely enough room for the cab to pass after it dropped me. I saw Pat's unmarked car just down the block. Took a real detective to find a parking space on this street before nine a.m.

His call had come in just after eight. I was already up and showered and shaved, sitting in the kitchenette in my underwear, eating the eggs and bacon I'd cooked up, drinking the coffee I'd brewed, as I read the *News*. Slow news day—neither the killer nor myself had killed anybody.

"Need to see you now," the Captain of Homicide said. Nothing friendly in his voice, but nothing unfriendly either. Strictly business.

"At your office?"

"No," he said, and gave me an address that I recognized at once. A chill worse than the one waiting outside for me crawled up my back like a stampede of spiders.

"Tell me," I said.

"No. You come see for yourself. I want you here ASAP, Mike."

"Okay," I said.

Well, now I was here. In front of the white-washed building with the green shutters and black ironwork. The two cops on the sidewalk were in rain slickers, ready for what was coming. I was in my trenchcoat and hat, but not ready for what waited for me up a flight of stairs. The cops were expecting me and waved me inside, and I went up.

The kid across the shared landing, Shack, in T-shirt and jeans, was sitting against the closed door of his own apartment with his legs hugged to himself, his head with its nest of curls angled down. He was sobbing, the tears making melting-wax trails on his bony face. He was curled up, as if trying to retreat inside himself, his position nearly fetal. He didn't seem to notice me.

A veteran harness bull stood guard next to the door opposite. He nodded and jerked his head for me to go on in. The door was ajar.

Pat met me, but left room to see past him. When I'd had a look, he held up the MICHAEL HAMMER INVESTIGATIONS business card and said, "Tell me why she had this, Mike."

I brushed by him and went over to the little work area on the braided rug. The lab boys weren't here yet, so she was all alone, just her and all those books surrounding her. In an oversize man's T-shirt turned into a petite girl's mini-length sleep apparel, she was seated Indian-style on the pillow and slumped onto the sawed-off table, head next to the typewriter, a small black powder-burned entry wound in her right temple. No exit wound visible, her head obviously resting on it.

Pat materialized next to me. "Bullet went in one temple and

out the other. Ninety-degree angle again."

By the open fingers of her right hand, its palm up, was a .22 Smith and Wesson Escort.

Bitterly, Pat said, "Does he get a discount, you think, buying so many of the goddamn things?"

I wanted to drop down there and take her into my arms and stroke her hair and soothe her, there there, there there, but it wouldn't do her any good, would it? The only thing I could do for her now was to stop the madman who'd done this evil thing, and much as I would have liked him to suffer the months of agony of the disease that was eating him and turning him ever more insane, I knew that his end had to come soon, very soon, before he took any more lives in what was clearly a psycho's game, now.

But silently I promised this girl something, this sweet smart kid with brains deserving of so much more than a bullet, who'd had all of her life ahead of her when I last saw her, only neither of us knew that span could be measured in hours. Marcy Bloom would never get the chance to really bloom, would she? So I promised her he would suffer, and that it wouldn't be quick.

We looked down at the girl, so young, so dead.

My lips were back over my teeth but it wasn't really a smile. "He's sticking it in our ass, Pat. Telling us to go screw ourselves royal. The Borensen kill might have passed for somebody really blotting himself out, the similarities between his death and Foster's just coincidental, or maybe an admission of guilt by Leif that he murdered his future father-in-law. But this time, the killer's staged a suicide for no reason other than to tell us it *isn't* a suicide."

"What this is," Pat said, "is a signature."

"Oh yeah. He signed this one all right, autographed the goddamn thing, and he's somewhere laughing himself silly at us.

The kind of laughter you don't hear outside a madhouse."

Pat was nodding. "So he's gone way over the edge, our hitman's hitman. Gone from professional to amateur."

"That's one way to look at it. But he's a *kill-crazy* amateur with cool professional skills. That makes him all kinds of dangerous."

"No argument, chum." He held up the little white card with the little black letters again. "Now, what was Marcy Bloom doing with your business card?"

"I was here yesterday evening."

"Kind of young for you."

I gave him a look. "I wasn't her type, Pat. She was Richard Blazen's co-author on that tell-all memoir he was writing. I spent several hours with her going over reams of transcripts and notes, looking for the name of Borensen's mob connection."

His eyes briefly flared. "And did you find it?"

I told him I had, and that I'd confronted Joey Pep at the Peppermint Lounge after leaving here last night. I said that Pepitone admitted that Borensen had been in the Bonetti family's pocket since the then-actor was peddling drugs among the Broadway crowd. I kept the talk about the family's contract-killer "specialist" to myself. Not ready to show Pat *all* my cards just yet.

"The Borensen/Bonetti connection could be useful," Pat said, "in a tangential way."

"You mean, in taking down the Bonettis."

"Yeah. And Joey has problems of his own. That famous club of his is on the verge of getting shuttered—losing its liquor license. They had an incident that won't help last night."

"Oh?"

He nodded. "Somebody driving by called it in. Nasty brouhaha between some guys out in front of the place. Two Peppermint Lounge bouncers got bounced to the hospital. They're still there, but they aren't talking." He gave me a sly smile. "That must have gone down after you left, huh, Mike?"

"Must have."

He pushed his hat back on his head. "The Bonettis catching flak is all well and good, but it doesn't get us any closer to your middle-of-the-night caller."

That gave me an opening to reveal some other cards to Pat. Putting him on a slow but worthwhile track while I was taking a faster one was a solid way to hedge my bets in the hunt for the Specialist. Yeah, capital "S"—I had something to call the son of a bitch now, at least.

So I told Pat about Dr. Beech and the disease that was taking down our killer in its own good time.

"Phasger's Syndrome?" he said, frowning. "Never heard of it… but it sure sounds like hell on earth."

"Even that's too good for this prick. But with a court order, you can get that list out of Dr. Beech, of the others who've made twenty-five-grand 'contributions.' They're all pay-offs for contract killings, of course. You can clear a slew of cases out of your unsolved homicides file, and maybe get a line on our psychotic hitman."

Head cocked, Pat was giving me a narrow-eyed look I knew too well. "How long have you been sitting on this information, Mike?"

"Since yesterday is all. I wasn't holding it back, buddy. Just hadn't got around to telling you yet."

His hands were on his hips. "Well, that's swell, Mike. 'Cause I would hate to have to haul you in on obstruction of justice charges."

"If you think I don't want this bastard found, Pat, you're crazier than he is."

"Well, one of us is. I've seen that look on your face before, Mike. Too many times. You want him for yourself. You want him in front of your .45, primed for one of your fancy self-defense pleas. Not this time. You can help us, and we'll be glad to have you—I for one appreciate your skills and acumen. But we're talking about a killer that could potentially lead us to taking down one of this city's five major crime families. If that happens, the death of this girl can maybe mean something, that something *good* will come of it. No, Mike, this time it's got to be by the book."

"No problems, old buddy. Strictly by the book."

The Old Testament.

"Listen, Pat," I said, "I don't see any of the Bloom girl's boxes of research materials. You want to build a case against the killer and/or the Bonettis, you'll want those. They turned out to be Marcy Bloom's life's work. Were they in the bedroom?"

He shook his head; this was all news to him. "No. The only materials are those few scattered things on that makeshift desk of hers."

I thumped his chest with a forefinger, just hard enough for some emphasis. "You need to canvass this building and at least the adjacent two, and the ones right across the street. When you have a time of death from the M.E., that'll help narrow it. But there were nine full boxes of those transcripts, and somebody had to carry them out of here, and down two flights out to the street. Load them in a car or whatever. By now those boxes and their contents will be destroyed, but you *may* get yourself a description of the killer."

"We already have that."

I blinked at him. "What?"

"I *will* put that canvass in motion, Mike, that makes a lot of sense. But that kid across the way saw the guy."

The lab boys and photographer were coming in, and we headed past them, to talk to Shack.

"This boy found the body," Pat said, just before we moved onto the landing, "shortly before seven. He often went in early and made coffee and sometimes breakfast for the girl. She'd leave the door unlocked for him."

The young man wasn't crying now, but he looked as dejected as a dog left along a roadside by a family moving on without him. The little landing was getting crowded, so Pat sent the uniformed man inside for now.

"Stand up, son," Pat said.

The kid struggled to his feet, each limb of his bony frame moving a little slower than the last. He was still in the peace symbol T-shirt and ancient jeans, his feet bare.

"This is Michael Hammer," Pat said, gesturing my way. "He's an investigator helping us—"

I said, "We've met. Shack helped Miss Bloom and me go through all those research materials."

"Ah," Pat said.

A sudden thought gripped me and I leaned near my friend, whispering, "Shack here might be able to testify to what we discovered in those transcripts."

Pat gave me a knowing nod, then turned back to the kid.

"Son, would you tell Mr. Hammer what you saw last night?"

"Can I *trust* him?" the kid blurted, flashing me a wary look. What was that about?

"You can," Pat assured him. "Just go over it again, please."

"Sure." He turned his narrow, angular face toward me; his eyes were bloodshot. "Around one a.m. last night, I heard knocking. *Loud* knocking. I, uh, cracked the door to see what was going on."

I said to Pat, "He does that." Then to Shack, I said, "Stop for a moment and describe him."

He nodded. "Okay. About five ten, eleven. Big but no giant. Kind of a Mr. Businessman type—dark suit, tie, hat. Hardly anybody wears a hat any more."

He was saying this to two guys in hats.

Pat asked, "Can you give me any more of a description than that?"

"Yes, sir. I got a real good look at him. Oval face, kind of a pug nose, wide-set dark eyes, small mouth. Short dark hair. Glasses, heavy plastic frames. Pale. Definitely not a guy who gets much sun, y'know?"

"All right," I said. "Get back to your story."

"Right. So, the guy was knocking for the umpteenth time, and I was about to go out there and tell him he'd better leave before he got himself in trouble... but then Marcy was there, in the doorway. She was trusting like that. Very open girl. Of course, that's the vibe down here. It's not like anywhere else in the city, the Village, you know?"

"We know," Pat said. "Go on."

"Well, this guy says to her, 'I'm sorry to bother you so late, Miss

Bloom, but Mr. Hammer asked me to pick up some materials that you and he worked with this evening.' There was some more talk that I didn't get, but finally she nodded and let him in. Shut the door, and I shut mine."

So that was why the kid didn't know whether or not to trust me—the killer had posed as my representative.

I asked, "Did you hear anything else last night? Like the guy leaving? Or maybe going up and down the stairs? Or most importantly—something that might have been a *gunshot*?"

He shook his head through all of that.

"You hear a lot of noises in the city," Shack said, shrugging. "Even in the Village. I guess... I guess not all the vibes down here are good."

"I guess not," I said.

"Son," Pat said, "would you be willing to come to my office and take a look through some mug books? We can start with individuals who we already suspect may be working as professional killers."

The bloodshot eyes grew wide. "Is *that* who killed Marcy? Some kind of... hitman?"

"It's too early for speculation," Pat said, which was a lie obviously. "We can give you a ride to and from. Could you be ready in half an hour?"

"Sure. *Anything* to get the freak that did this."

"If need be," Pat offered, "I can talk to your boss where you work, so you don't get in trouble."

"Oh, I don't work anywhere. I'm a painter. Like Jackson Pollock. I'll have a gallery show one of these days. Till then Mom and Dad kind of... underwrite me."

"It's an investment," I said.

"I think so," Shack said, a little defensively.

Then he disappeared into his apartment.

"What's going to become of these hippie kids?" Pat wondered aloud.

"Well, it's official."

"What is?"

"You're an old fart."

We grinned at each other. We could use it.

"Did that boy love her, Mike?"

"He had a terrible crush on her, even though it was misplaced."

"She wouldn't have anything to do with him?"

"Oh, no, she was friendly with him. Took advantage a little, knowing he was sweet on her."

"*Now* who sounds like an old fart?"

I laughed. "Thing is, she was gay. Or did you know that already?"

His eyes flared momentarily. "No. We should probably ask around and look into her girl friends or girl friend. They might know something."

I gave a fatalistic shrug. "I doubt it. Marcy didn't know her killer. But there'll be some sad gals in the Village tonight." I tugged my hat brim down for the coming rain. "You need me any longer, Pat?"

He shook his head. "No. But I would like to know, Mike—are you going to work with me on this? How about it? Can we do this one together? Or does it have to be a damn race again?"

I let him have half a grin. "Come on, buddy, you know I'm a solo act."

"Yeah? Tell that to Velda."

"Okay, so I sometimes work with a beautiful doll. You couldn't pass the physical. Hey, I gave you the Dr. Beech lead, which you and your army of brilliant scientific types can handle much quicker and faster than an old-time flatfoot like me ever could. You're welcome, by the way, for all the cases you'll close."

His gaze dripped of suspicion. "What are you going to be doing?"

"Trying another route. A shorter one." I put a hand on his shoulder. "But if I don't make it, buddy—if our killer turns out to be a badder ass than yours truly—promise me you'll find this bastard. But it'll take a hell of a lot of digging."

"That's our specialty," Pat said. His smile wasn't big, but it had plenty of friendship in it. "But don't die on me just yet, you big slob."

"I'll see what I can do."

I started heading down the stairs.

He called after me: "What *are* you going to do, Mike? What have you got in mind, to beat me and the NYPD to this guy?"

"Nothing much," I said up to him. "Just giving the bastard some bait."

"What kind of bait?"

"Me."

At the office, I called Velda from the phone on her own desk.

I said, "Have you cheated on me with Billy Batson yet?"

"You'd deserve that, you louse. If you don't give me the go-ahead to get out of this place, they'll be locking me up next door in their Laughing Academy."

"Now, easy, kitten. This thing is really heating up. I need you to stay put and keep an eye on our little pal."

"Damnit, Mike, don't squeeze me out like this!"

"You have to give me room on this one, doll."

"You mean, like, I have to give you enough rope?"

I removed anything light from my voice; nothing was left but a deadly edge. "Listen to me, Velda. This guy is on the rampage, and he may be the craziest, smartest son of a bitch we've ever taken on."

Her voice went hushed. "Why, what's happened now, Mike?"

I brought her quickly up to speed on everything that had gone down since she and I last spoke.

"That poor kid," she said about Marcy, the sadness in her voice revealing her depth of feeling despite never having met the girl. "Oh, Mike. Somebody's got to die for that. And die very hard."

"I'm on it. But you need to stay right where you are. Both you and Billy could be in danger. The killer is tying off loose ends, so you need to stay on your guard. I would give decent odds that he may try to strike at me through you."

"Mike, that's not going to happen. Not with me here in this damn fortress…"

"The Alamo was a fortress, too, kid."

"Actually it was a church. And I wish you'd let me do more in this, Mike, than just pray for you."

But she told me she'd do as I asked, and that she loved me. I echoed the last, then hung up, hoping I'd live through this to see her again.

CHAPTER FIFTEEN

I figured my next move was to corner Joey Pep again, and tell him his high-priced hitman had knocked off an innocent girl last night. Make him see that his so-called Specialist had gone off the rails and needed stopping, right now. Maybe Pepitone would see the wisdom of that and lead me to the bastard. Or maybe I'd have to give Joey a taste of what his bouncers got.

So what if the Bonettis got pissed at me over it? I'd had mob trash pissed at me before. Sure, they knew where to find me. But I knew where to find them.

If memory served, the Peppermint Lounge opened at eleven a.m., typical for a Manhattan bar, but also to accommodate the tourist crowd who hadn't heard the twist craze was over. Pepitone still had his office in the backroom, so from my desk phone I called over there and asked for him. He wasn't in yet. Usually showed around one. You wanna leave a message? I said no thanks, and I didn't leave a name, either.

I'd barely hung up when the phone rang. I answered and heard Pat's voice, hushed yet anxious.

"Mike, can you get over here?"

There was nothing official in his tone.

"What is it now?" I asked. "Did that kid find somebody in a mug book?"

"Just get over here, Mike. Please."

Please, yet!

"Okay," I said, hung up, grabbed my hat and trenchcoat and headed out into an afternoon where the sky had deepened from gray to black, like God was in a bad mood. Maybe He was hungry, too, because it sure as hell sounded like His stomach was growling.

Pat's office door was open. He was in his shirtsleeves and a loosened tie behind his desk, and he looked haggard. He waved me in and said, "Shut it."

I did, then went over, tossed my hat on his desk, and slung myself into the chair opposite him. He already had coffee waiting. I sipped mine. Milk and sugar. Perfect.

"What can I do for you, Captain?"

"I'd like your help."

"Any time, buddy."

He sat forward, his voice soft yet with an underlying edge. "I need you to back me up on something. Something that's a little… dicey. Something more along, you know—*your* lines."

I was interested, but couldn't resist needling him a little. "What happened to 'by the book?'"

His smile was rumpled and maybe a shade embarrassed. "We'll leave it open on my desk. Face down."

I nodded. "So spill."

His eyes narrowed. "We had that kid in here for an hour. Looking at mug books. He came up with nothing. I was grasping at straws, I admit. So I showed him a wire photo the LAPD sent me just two hours ago."

"Why did the LAPD do that?"

He leaned back in his swivel chair, the gray-blue eyes troubled but steady. "You know, Mike, you're not the only detective in this town."

"Well, it's a big town." I was lighting up a Lucky. "Bound to be a few. Maybe even some on this department."

"Generous of you to admit."

I waved out the match. "Let me guess. You've been contacting big city police departments, chatting up friends working homicide, guys you met at police conventions maybe. And you ran the profile past them."

Something flashed in his eyes. "What profile would that be?"

I blew a smoke ring, feeling cocky. "Guys who had small, seemingly legit businesses, like one-man insurance agencies or travel agent set-ups or maybe accountants, who got pulled in on suspicion of a killing, but walked. Guys whose businesses were legit but barely making it, and that just might be fronts for contract killers to hide behind between jobs. Guys who, finally, booked it out of town when the cops were getting on to them."

He gave me half a smile and a whole laugh. "Okay, so I'm not the only detective in town, either. You're right, Mike. I wanted to see who else our hitman's hitman might have brought in to join his stable of hired guns."

"And you found a possible. Or rather the LAPD did."

He nodded emphatically. "But we may have caught a bigger fish than I figured."

The wire photo he handed over to me showed, in typical front and side views, a blank-eyed, square-faced guy with short dark hair and regular features. Name: Dennis Clark, thirty-five, six one, two hundred pounds. He had the bland, clean-cut good looks of a Madison Avenue ad man. Native of Southern California.

"This goes back five years," I said.

Pat nodded again. "The profile is the same, but Dennis Clark has been in Manhattan, running a small insurance agency, for just that long."

"Not a recent import."

"Not at all. And if he's hiding, it's in plain sight. Took me about three minutes to get his home address."

I sat forward. "So maybe this is our man. The top of the food chain."

An eyebrow went up. "I think he is. And there's more than just theory behind that."

I tossed him back the wire photo. "You mean, that kid Shack identified him?"

"Well… yes and no."

"You might want to break that down."

Pat sipped some coffee, shrugged. "It was 'yes' at first. Kid made the guy. He had to study it a while, and of course that wire photo like all wire photos is crappy quality. But then he started nodding and tapped it with his finger and said it was the man he saw go into the girl's apartment. He was sure it was him."

"So why aren't you out there picking Dennis Clark up?"

His smile had a bitter twist. "Because when I told that kid that we'd be bringing Clark in for a show-up, he got nervous. Started asking questions, like, 'Will he know that I identified him?' And I had to tell him, yes, eventually, if this made it to trial, he would have to testify. He'd have to point Clark out in the courtroom as the man he saw go into Marcy Bloom's last night. That is, if Clark indeed was who the kid saw. We hadn't even had a show-up yet."

I was ahead of him. "And that's where the 'no' half of 'yes and no' comes in. The kid suddenly didn't recognize the suspect. Got unsure of himself, then finally said, 'I don't think that's the guy,' or words to that effect. And hustled his skinny scared ass out of here."

"Like they say in the Village," Pat commented bitterly, "it's a bummer."

"It's a bummer, all right. The kid was nuts about that girl, but it's not hard to rationalize saving your own skin. Helping haul her killer to justice doesn't bring the girl back."

Pat pounded a fist on his desk. "If that hippie hadn't retracted his ID, I'd be over at Clark's apartment house right now, with men on the street and all over that building. And I'd be going in there heavy and taking him down. Personally."

"Arresting him, you mean."

Pat frowned at me. "If he cooperates. If he doesn't… he goes down all the way. He goes down hard."

"Now you're talking."

He sat forward, frustration tightening his face. "Only, Mike—I can't do that. I don't even have enough to bring the S.O.B. in for questioning. All I have is a wire photo from L.A. that *might* back up a theory I have that could just be a wild hair up my ass. I have a witness ID that's been withdrawn, worthless. What if I go there, and bring Dennis Clark in, and I'm wrong? Well, I'm getting a little old to pound a beat on Staten Island, and too young for early retirement."

My grin must have been horrible; I was glad I didn't have to look at it. "Old buddy, you are screwed sideways. You really don't have enough to bring him in. You don't even have enough to *talk* to him. Anything that came of it would get tossed out by some holier-than-thou judge."

"You're wrong, Mike."

"I am?"

"It would never make it past the D.A." He leaned both elbows on his desk and looked right at me. "But what if I told *you* about all this? Off-duty. Over beers, maybe. Since we're old friends and you're involved in the case."

"Stranger things have happened."

"And you tell me you're going over there to shake the truth out of this new suspect. I of course would tell you not to, try to stop you, and finally insist if you're determined to talk to Mr. Clark— as a part of your private investigation into the case—that I have to come along."

I considered it, then said, "You might get in a little hot water over that. But not boiling."

"What do you think, Mike?"

"I think… what are we waiting for?"

The somewhat pricey neighborhood in Upper Manhattan called Washington Heights was home to seemingly countless apartment buildings, Dennis Clark's among them. The nine stories of rust-brick on the corner of West 187th Street and Cabrini bore a stark prewar modernity, though the inset twin front doors with their brass-trim and geometric designs, surrounded by panels of pink marble and two square windows above, formed the mouth of a startled Art-Deco face that gaped at your approach.

We took my car, since Pat was supposedly tagging along with me, though it was actually vice versa. It wouldn't seem like he was trying to keep me out of trouble if he drove me here. We snagged a nice close parking place, which was a small miracle and a relief, as the sky looked as if it were made of billowing black smoke from a terrible fire, though rain was what it promised.

There was no doorman outside and no sign-in post inside, just a small lobby with a marble floor and more '30s-modern trimmings. We walked to a bank of two elevators where Pat punched UP. In our trenchcoats and hats, we looked no more like cops than guys in ten-gallon numbers and chaps did cowboys. Behind us, through the closed doors, came a sudden machine-gun downpour.

"We just made it," I said.

Pat barely noticed. He had the expression of a father driving his thirteen-year-old sheltered son to a dance with a fifteen-year-old girl wearing too much lipstick.

"I want him alive," Pat said, staring me down. "Understand, Mike? Alive."

"Yeah, yeah, breathing and everything. Christ, Pat, we don't even know for sure he's the guy and you've got me shooting him already."

"Since when were you fussy?"

Despite this, on the self-service elevator, Pat got out his .38

service revolver and shoved it in his right raincoat pocket. I did the same with my .45.

Clark's apartment was on the eighth floor, a few doors to the left of where the elevator deposited us. Pat took the lead. He was poised to knock when I whispered, "Take no chances, buddy."

Pat nodded, and put his back to the wall nearest the knob and I did the same to the other, each of us with a hand in our right pockets gripping a gun. He reached his left fist over and knocked.

We heard movement within.

"Mr. Clark," Pat said, loud but in an even, unthreatening manner. "NYPD Homicide. We'd like to speak to you, sir."

A few seconds passed, and Pat seemed about to say something else when the flurry of bullets punched through the wood of the door, accompanied by mini-bursts of thunder that the sky might have envied.

Though our backs were to the wall, literally and maybe figuratively, we both ducked down anyway.

"Next time," I said tightly, "skip the 'Homicide.'"

"Point well-taken."

We both heard something in there.

A window was being forced up and open, confirmed by the abrupt loudness of a raging storm that had been muffled till now.

"He's going out," I said to Pat, across the bullet-puckered doorway.

"Where the hell *to*? We're eight stories up, man!"

"The fire escape."

Pat frowned. "There's no fire escape out that window. It's around the corner on the other side of the building."

No more time for talk. I didn't think I'd be at any risk of more gunfire coming through that door. So I kicked it open in a splintering crunch, pushed the damaged result aside, and rushed in. With .45 in hand but shedding the trenchcoat and hat, I crossed the living room of a modern apartment toward a window that yawned wide and spewed rain to discourage me.

From the doorway, Pat yelled, "Mike, what the hell...?"

"Find something useful to do," I told him.

"I'll call for back-up," he said, and was gone.

I peered out around the window frame and there, through the driving sheets, was a man in a dark, already dripping suit hugging the brick, his shoes angled sideways to take advantage of the six-inch ledge of cement. He faced away from me as he moved incrementally toward the corner of the building, around which the fire escape waited.

Just barely peeking out, my face streamed with the sky's tears, my upper clothes already soaked. I leaned out to get a better look at him, specifically to see if he'd put his gun away.

He hadn't.

It was in his right hand, and flat against the brick. In the limited visibility of the downpour, I could tell only that it was an automatic, a nine millimeter possibly or maybe a .45.

But the gun was, no question, slowing him down. It gave him only one hand to secure purchase on the brick, and he was inching his feet along. I'd be inching along too if I carried my .45 out there. I could shoot him from the window, but Pat wanted him alive, and I owed my friend that much. Anyway, if this was the Specialist, I didn't want to give him the easy mercy of a .45

slug in the head. He had much worse coming.

So I stuffed the .45 in my waistband and slipped out of the already sopping suitcoat. Then I leaned out into the torrent, my fingers testing the slipperiness of the narrow ledge, and it seemed more wet than slick.

Right?

Then I was on the cement tightrope myself, pressed against that building like it was the most beautiful, desirable woman in creation, my fingers clutching where brick met mortar, my feet turned sideways like a figure in an Egyptian hieroglyphic.

Out here came a rush of sudden cold, and the slanting rain whipped my back with surprising power. I was drenched now. But with both hands free, I made quicker, surer progress than my quarry, though once I got overconfident and my foot slipped off into nothing at all and I froze against the beautiful woman and clung for my life.

The barrage of rain created a pounding din that seemed like the loudest thing on earth until thunder like terrible cannon fire made something insignificant out of it.

Yet still I edged, getting closer. Only he was getting ever nearer to that corner, and if he beat me there, and made it around, then when I did the same, who could say what I might be facing?

The sky was roaring with laughter now, raucous belly laughs, as one man pursued another at the rate of an inch for every step, a snail chasing a snail. And yet finally he made it to that corner, and as he slipped around he saw me for the first time, his eyes flashing at me before he disappeared.

What could I do but keep going?

I was passing windows on other apartments, but a man on a six-inch ledge can't kick the glass in or even hurl himself through. The former might send him toppling backward, the latter would have him bouncing off, not through, the window, tumbling back into the abyss.

And the sky laughed deep.

Then I was there, at the corner myself. I stopped to catch my breath, but taking air in through my nose, not risking letting rain in through my mouth—a coughing fit right now could be fatal. I was a sodden excuse for a human, the moisture half-blinding me now, streaming down my face, weeping for me. But I'd reached my goal.

Rounding the corner was a trick in itself, but I didn't make the turn completely, instead froze there hugging the central sharpness of brick.

He'd made it to the fire escape. *He was on it.* He was waiting. Even in the rain I could see that this man wore the face in the LAPD wire photo. This was almost certainly the Specialist. He had said he would take me on and beat me at my own game.

And he was about to.

Maybe madness *had* taken him, as I'd speculated, because he was laughing back at the sky, laughing at me, his demented eyes blinking away rain even as he brought the automatic up to pick me off my perch. My hand fumbled for the .45 in my waistband and I waited for the gunshot…

… and it came.

Like more thunder, but sharper, only I felt nothing—*he'd missed!* My eyes struggled open under their cargo of raindrops and saw him tottering at the edge of the fire escape. He hadn't missed, someone else had fired, and the bullet caught him in the shoulder but the shock of it sent the automatic in now loose fingers dropping harmlessly into the maw of the storm.

Then he fell into it, too.

Screaming, but the gods laughing thunderously at him made it sound small even before it receded with him to the pavement where he splattered like a tomato flung at a wall.

Down on the street, a barely visible figure in a trenchcoat pointed up. Maybe a gun was in its hand. And I was pretty sure it was Pat. Then from behind me a voice called over the rain, "Get back here, mister! *Careful!* I'll help you in…"

Somehow I managed, and a frumpy woman about forty, as plain as a paint can, helped me in, and I never saw a female who looked better.

I was sitting on the floor in a puddle, some of which I may have made myself, near the now-closed window, still breathing hard, when somebody knocked on the door. My hostess went and answered it and Pat came quickly in and right over to me.

He kneeled down, face taut with concern, hat shedding water. Put a hand on my shoulder.

"You okay, buddy?" he said.

"I thought you wanted him alive."

He gave me what they call a rueful grin. "Yeah, well, priorities. Somebody's ass needed saving."

The woman came over and said her husband was about my size, and brought me fresh underwear and a suit they were planning to give to Goodwill. I accepted the offering. Frankly, the suit looked decent enough that I might keep it.

In a nice warm bathroom, I toweled off and got into the threads, then gave the gal a kiss on the cheek and went down the hall to see Pat, where he was in Dennis Clark's apartment.

The place was very modern in a sterile kind of way, with not a picture on the wall or book on a shelf, though it had a nice twenty-four inch TV and an impressive sound system with a record collection running to Mingus and Davis. There were clothes, including some expensive conservative suits, and food in the fridge, import beer, deli cold cuts, milk and so on. But no bills or other correspondence, the stuff that lives are made of.

Pat did find two things of interest. One was a little black book, the kind a guy keeps the names and numbers of his favorite females in. Only this little black book had the names of men, and just a handful—a very specific handful.

"The three assassins," Pat said, "who came after you. Names, phone numbers, addresses."

"It's impressive, watching your detecting skills at work."

A few minutes later he came up with a bank book from under some clothes in a dresser drawer.

He thumbed through it, then whistled slow. "Dennis Clark has a hundred grand and change in savings, Mike."

"Yeah, well, you can't take it with you."

Outside the storm was dissipating. The machine-gunning was tap-dancing now, and the view out the window was gray, not black. Distant sirens announced the cavalry coming, just as late as in the movies.

"Doesn't it feel a little convenient, Pat? A little easy?"

He made a face. "It's the guy, Mike. Don't be a sore loser."

"Sore loser, how?"

He grinned at me. "Because for once I beat you to it."

CHAPTER SIXTEEN

Several days later, we were having coffee after lunch at the Blue Ribbon, seated at the corner table in the niche of celebrity photos—Velda and me and Hy Gardner, who was heading back to Florida later this afternoon.

"Things are pretty much back to normal," Velda was saying to Hy. She was in a light blue silk blouse today and a dark blue pencil skirt, and looked sexier than Ann Corio at the end of her act.

The columnist looked at her skeptically over the glasses halfway down his droopy nose. "'Normal' being a relative term where Mike Hammer is concerned."

"Normal," I said, patting my partner's hand, "is having Velda back at her desk, where she belongs."

She smirked at me. "That's your version of barefoot and pregnant, right?"

I raised my hands in surrender. Some battles just aren't worth fighting.

"You know, Mike," Hy said, that naturally dour puss of his at odds with the laughter in his eyes, "you're really slipping."

"Am I?"

Velda said, "Oh, I don't know, Hy. If he was slipping, then the other day he'd have been splashed all over the sidewalk like our hitman friend."

Hy sipped coffee, then said to me, "What I mean is—the biggest contract killing ring since Murder, Incorporated, and you let *Pat* take it to the finish line? It's not like you, Mike."

Velda said, "Oh, my fearless leader's not satisfied. He's still snooping around the edges of the case, like a dog looking for the right tree."

"With the bad guy in the morgue?" Hy said. Right now there was something pixie-ish in the middle-aged man's expression. "Since when did you care about loose ends, Mike?"

"This whole thing has been about loose ends," I said. "Maybe you shouldn't head home to the beach and the sunshine just yet. I might have a story for you that'll put you back on the front page."

Hy waved that away. "It's been a long time since I worked the crime beat, Mike. Those two Broadway musicals I covered this trip were criminal enough."

"Well," Velda said, "maybe Gwen Foster's new one will make your next trip worthwhile."

"Oh?"

I said, "Yeah, she called this morning. She's going to back the production herself that her late father and the unlamented Leif were going to mount."

"That girl's going places," Hy said. He checked his watch. "And so am I. I need to get back to the Plaza to pack and check out before heading to LaGuardia."

He grabbed the check and gave Velda a kiss on the cheek, and headed out.

She and I had another cup of coffee.

"Mike," she said softly, "why aren't you satisfied that this thing is over? Pat seems to be."

"It's those damn loose ends, kitten."

"Too many of them."

"No. Not enough."

She frowned, but didn't ask for an explanation, which was fine, because I wasn't sure I had one.

I flagged a cab and we took a ride to a certain corner on Lexington. It wasn't on the way to the office, but my excuse was that I wanted to pick up the magazines that Billy regularly held for me.

He was back at the old stand, literally, a small, distinctive figure in his old plaid cap and new padded jacket, replacing the one that got shot up. Colorful comic-book covers were on racks at right and left, and the best newsstand selection of papers, paperbacks, and periodicals in Manhattan was on festive display under the little roof.

The tallest Singer Midget gave me the stack of magazines with *Saga* on top and *Playboy* hidden half-way down, out of respect to Velda.

I said, "You don't look much the worse for wear, kiddo."

"Hey, Mike, I feel like a million bucks and change. It's like I took a rest cure!" Billy grinned at Velda on my arm, and there was a hint of lechery in it. "And best of all, I had me a real babe of a nurse."

She gave him a kiss on the forehead that must have made at least his day and probably his week. Then we caught another cab and headed back to our home base at the Hackard Building.

The afternoon went quickly. I had some insurance company paperwork to deal with that had piled up. Velda had stacks of mail to go through, and now and then she'd come into my office with a question or a menial task—sign this, check that.

"Hey, you got something today from that Dr. Beech," she said, waving an envelope at me.

"Wonder what this is," I said, taking it. "Pat should be dealing with him by now, going after those contract-kill donors. I don't see where I'd have anything to do with Dr. Beech at this point."

She shrugged and went out, moving in that liquid way, like her bottom was operating on pistons. I took time out to watch. Some views you can't ever see too many times.

The letter from Beech did include a paragraph about cooperating with Pat, but mostly it was something else. Something that made me really smile. I tucked the letter away and tossed it on the desk and had a big old laugh that damn near rattled the blinds.

Velda stuck her head in. "What's so darn funny?"

"Nothing, doll. I just have a sick sense of humor."

She smirked. "Tell me something I don't know."

I reached for the phone and soon had Pat on the line.

"What is it, Mike? Kind of busy here."

"Why, is there a line of cops going out your door wanting to pat you on the back? Or maybe you have to see the Commissioner to hear about a medal or commendation for service above the—"

"Or maybe I'm just trying to live down saving Mike Hammer's tail. You think there aren't guys on the force who wouldn't have liked to see you fall off that ledge? That would've been the splat heard round the department."

He had a point.

"Just a couple of things I'd like to go over," I said. "Some things aren't tracking for me."

"Okay." Slight impatience in it.

"The other day, I got a look at that bank book you found. That hundred grand was deposited in a new account, just a few days before. Doesn't that make your antennae tingle?"

There was a shrug in his voice. "Not particularly. I'm sure guys in Clark's business move money around all the time. Is that all, Mike?"

"No. There's the little black book you found. It only has three entries in it."

"So what?"

"Well, start with this—what the hell kind of address book has only three names in it?"

"There's no law that says it has to have more."

"Hell, Pat, don't you think it's just a little suspicious? Kind of goddamn convenient? That it had the three names we wanted to see, and nothing or nobody else?"

"No. Those were the hitmen Clark recruited from out of town. Maybe there would have been more, eventually."

"My middle-of-the-night caller didn't *have* an 'eventually.' Not a few weeks away from that Phasger's Syndrome kicking in."

"Well, I just don't see any significance."

"Think! You need to have the coroner check and see if Clark had the disease."

"There's already been an autopsy, which is no picnic when the deceased hit cement from eight stories up, and nothing came up. Except maybe a few lunches."

"But was the coroner *looking* for Phasger's?"

"Mike—"

"I went down to Greenwich Village earlier today. Stopped by the Bloom girl's building. Did you know that kid moved out?"

"Actually, I did."

"And you didn't mention it to me? Christ!"

"Mike, you aren't on the Homicide Squad, last time I checked. But for your information, yes, our hippie pal ran out of headquarters scared shitless and skedaddled out of that apartment. Can you blame him?"

I laid on the sarcasm. "Surely he would have seen the media coverage of how a brave captain of homicide had brought the Borensen case to a successful, exciting conclusion..."

"Mike, Shack moved out that same afternoon. *Before* things came to a conclusion. Just kind of... disappeared. The building manager says these hippie kids are always moving suddenly. They don't stay in one place long."

"Ever consider that if the kid has 'disappeared,' maybe he's dead? Gone swimming, maybe—the kind where you don't come up for air until gas bloat *brings* you up? Maybe Shack's another loose end that got tied off, and if so, Clark wasn't our man."

"*Clark wasn't our man?* Damn! What the hell are you *talking* about, Mike?"

"I'm saying it smells like a set-up. You were handed just the right items, Pat—the bank book, the address book, and the perfect patsy, the perfect *corpse*, to make this case look closed."

"You need to tame that imagination of yours, buddy."

"And you need to *develop* an imagination, Captain Chambers!"

He hung up on me.

I called out to Velda. "*Damnit!* He hung up on me!"

From her desk, she called back: "Imagine that."

Just before five, Velda leaned in the doorway between our offices and said, "How about a home-cooked meal tonight, Handsome? I think you know how to get to my apartment. But it does require the mastery of an elevator."

From behind my desk, which was piled with paperwork, I said, "Okay, but let's make it a late supper. Look for me around nine. I'm going to stay late and catch up on this work."

She nodded her okay and went out. From the connecting doorway, she leaned back in with a wry smile and called, "I'll make sure to lock up good and proper."

I heard the outer door close behind her and the appropriate clicks, then got up, walked out there and undid the secondary lock. I returned to the inner office and cleared everything off my desk except Dr. Beech's letter. I slipped out of my suit coat and slung it over the desk chair, then got the .45 out, checked the action, and returned it to its home under my left arm.

Then I stretched out on my back on the black-leather couch along the side wall, to the left as you entered. My hands were intertwined behind my neck, and I used an arm of the couch as a pillow, my elbows winged. I had a good view of the door between this office and the outer one. The couch was well-padded and I'd had many a nice snooze here.

But I was wide awake—relaxing, relaxed, but alert.

It would end where it began.

Velda had been gone maybe half an hour when I heard the door open and the footsteps move cautiously toward my inner chamber. I'd left the connecting door open. I wanted to make it easy for him.

The man, rather tall in a well-tailored charcoal suit, stood framed in the doorway, a Garcia-Beretta nine millimeter in his right hand. No gloves. He had a narrow, smooth face with unmemorable features, his eyes dark and cold, like polished stones.

Those eyes went to the desk first, then to me on the couch.

"Have a seat, Shack," I said.

He smiled just a little. I had a feeling that emotions were something that didn't run deep with him, at least emotions that required empathy or sympathy. That gave his face an unused look. A younger-than-it-was look. But he had *really* appeared young with that wig of shoulder-length brown curls helping him play hippie.

I said, "I figured you'd have a copy of the key that Woodcock made. And since you could defeat the secondary lock anyway, with your kind of skills, I just unlatched it for you. As a time-saving courtesy."

He nodded his thanks.

Then cautiously he made his way to the client's chair and with his free hand turned it toward me, then sat. He crossed his legs and rested the barrel of the nine millimeter on his knee.

I said, "I'm going to very slowly sit up and swing around. So we can make eye contact as we talk. Is that all right, Shack?"

He nodded.

I did so, positioning myself on the edge of the middle cushion. "How old are you really?"

The tiny smile again. "Thirty-five."

"You interest me, Shack. I'm going to use that name, because it's the only one I have for you. That okay?"

He nodded again.

I said, "Tell me a little about yourself."

"You must be joking, Hammer." The voice was somewhere between the hippie kid and the middle-of-the-night caller.

"No. I've encountered all kinds in my line of work. What's your story? Chapter and verse is fine, or condense it if you like."

He shook his head. The cold eyes blinked only rarely.

"Then do you mind if I take a stab? You were in the military. You're the right age for Korea, if you went right out of high school. You found out over there that killing people didn't bother you at all. In fact, you got a kick out of it. You came home with some medals and went to college on the G.I. bill. You took business courses."

The blank, unused face made it difficult to discern, but I detected the frown, which was mostly a tensing of the eyebrows. He really thought maybe I knew who he was and had found all this stuff out.

I continued: "You may have opened an insurance agency or some other small business, something white collar, no retail for

243

you. And then it dawned on you that you had a marketable skill, not to mention the college background to take that skill to a new level. How many years have you been killing people for profit, Shack?"

"Seven," he said.

"Not all of it here in New York. You were somewhere else for a while, things got hot, a change of name, a change of location, and you aligned yourself with the Bonettis."

The polished-stone eyes narrowed slightly. "You're shrewder than I expected, Hammer. You're smarter. I knew you were a ruthless killer, and good at it. But I admit it—I'm impressed."

I grinned at him. "Thanks. A few other questions, before we get to it, if that's all right?"

He nodded.

"How long," I asked, "were you Shack, the hippie kid across the way?"

"Five weeks, more or less."

"The purpose? No, let me try. It was several things. You wanted to get rid of Blazen's incriminating materials for Joey Pep. No wonder nobody heard or saw those boxes of research leave the apartment building—all you had to do was lug them across the landing into your own pad. And, too, you wanted to see how long it took me to track Marcy Bloom down. Of course you always intended, in your own good time, to kill her. She would make too important a witness for the cops, with all she knew about Blazen's digging. She was a loose end. And you do not like loose ends, do you, Shack?"

"I don't," he admitted.

"And that I don't understand. What's wrong with loose ends

in your situation? After all, that disease is going to kill you. Who cares if you're revealed as a hired killer? I mean, don't you see yourself as the greatest gun that ever shot some poor innocent kid? Like Marcy Bloom?"

No expression now. Blank. "Now you don't seem so smart, Hammer."

"Oh, you want me to think it through for you? How about this? If the cops get you, they'll stick you in a prison hospital where keeping you comfy will be a priority rating somewhere between changing shit-on sheets and emptying bedpans. You have a high-priced clinic lined up somewhere... maybe in Europe?"

The minuscule smile returned.

I laughed. "That's it! Somewhere with the best care, the best drugs, though as I understand it, there's not much ahead for you, no matter how much you spend, but horror."

The smile disappeared.

"Also," I said, "you figured to get me off-guard. You wanted me to buy what Captain Chambers did—that Dennis Clark was the mastermind. Really, Shack, that was pretty transparent—a hundred grand deposited a few days before, three solitary names in an address book. You left some of your things in that apartment, which I believe really was yours, but you took a lot with you. So I figure your man Dennis Clark came at your request to that apartment, to meet you on business. You gave him a key or let him in, then told him you had to step out for a while... whatever. You were the boss. He did as he was told. And you repaid his loyalty by setting him up for the kill. You'd told him that the cops were closing in, right? So that he'd blast away when they showed.

And the mastermind hitman would be dead. Anything you'd like to correct?"

He shook his head, a small motion.

"You know, I should have tipped sooner, at the Bloom girl's pad. You said you were a painter, but there was no coloration under your fingernails. But I thought the painting bit was a sham designed to get money out of your parents. That is, the imaginary parents of an imaginary hippie… Do you mind if I smoke, Shack? This is a tense situation, and it may calm me."

"No," he said sharply. "Don't smoke."

"I'm not going to throw an ashtray at you or anything, like I did your boy Woodcock. Oh, wait… I know. I get it. It's that ever-present smell of ashes that you experience. It's an early symptom. Getting more extreme, as time runs out, is it? Okay, to help you stay comfortable, Shack… I won't smoke."

"Thank you."

"I do have another theory I'd like to run past you, before we get to the fun-and-games portion of our program. I don't think you developed a stable of killers at all. Maybe Clark, but no one else. I think they may have thought that was what you were up to— but it wasn't. They were strictly here as game pieces in our little competition. You looked for people in your line of work who had done well. You brought them in and sicced them on me, one at a time. It would, as you said once, demonstrate whether or not I was worthy of your regard. And if one succeeded in killing me, perhaps you'd have found a successor. Someone you could turn your business over to. Just a thought."

He said nothing.

"One last question—when you shot at Billy that night, you had a perfect opportunity to take me out, too. Why didn't you?"

He lifted the nine mil and said, "Stand up."

I stood, slowly, arms at my side.

He placed the nine mil on the desk, within easy reach.

I grinned at him. "Just like the Old West, huh?"

"Just like that. Let's see how fast you really are, Hammer."

Traffic sounds outside my window were a reminder of a world that didn't know and didn't care what was happening here.

I said, "There's another possibility, Shack. It's possible that all you want from me is to kill you. That you'll be slower than me, intentionally, now that you're convinced I'm a worthy executioner. *That's* why you didn't kill me when you went after Billy—I'm your chosen suicide method. I'm your rope. Your razor. Your gun."

He reached for the nine mil and my .45 flew into my hand and thundered and the bullet carved a deep notch in my desk, missing his fingers by a fraction of an inch, as it sent the nine millimeter flying. The gun clunked to the floor somewhere, out of sight.

The man who wasn't really called Shack stood there shaking. The cordite in the air couldn't be helping that smell symptom of his.

"Do it," he said. "Goddamn you, Hammer. *Do it.*"

"You shouldn't have killed that girl in the Village, Shack. I couldn't care less about Leif Borensen. But Martin Foster was a good man. Only the last straw, my friend, the last goddamn straw, was Marcy Bloom. She just didn't deserve it."

I moved slowly toward him, .45 trained on him. His eyes were filling with the tears he'd been incapable of shedding for others.

He was shaking like a leaf. Or maybe a Leif. He didn't want to die, not really. But he knew it was his best option.

Then I was right on him, inches from him. "If I were to shoot you, Shack—and I'm not going to—I'd give it to you low and in the belly, where a .45 slug goes in small and comes out big, and it takes a long, long time to bleed out and die. It's what you're going to suffer when Phasger's kicks in, but in miniature. Only even that is too good for you."

I shoved the gun in his gut, its nose pressed deep.

"No, Shack, you get to take the full ride. You're going to prison, to some dismal ward, where nobody will give two shits that you are suffering. You'll get it all, the whole attack of your nervous system on itself—constant pain, the loss of comprehensible speech, bleeding from the eyes and God knows where else, feeding through an I.V., teeth falling out, blindness, and pain, so much pain, that even morphine will bring no mercy."

His hands flew between us and he clutched my Colt in both, its nose still deep in his belly, and he grinned at me maniacally as a thumb forced my finger on the trigger and the .45's explosion was muffled by his body as the slug thrust into and through him and took him down in a sudden well-dressed pile.

"You lose, Hammer. You l-lose."

I backed away, holstered the .45, and lighted up a cigarette. Then I reached for the letter from Dr. Beech. "Here's something interesting I got in the mail today."

I took out and unfolded the sheet and held it before the eyes of a man whose grotesque expression of a pain both physical and emotional was so exquisite, no words could do it justice. The veins of his neck bulged out in pale blue relief and the crazy wrenching that was tearing at his torn guts was eating at his mind, too, making his eyes bug out as if they might burst like balloons.

I said, "Maybe you can't see so well right now, so I'll summarize. You know, Dr. Beech has been on the verge of a breakthrough in Phasger's Syndrome for some time. Thanks largely to generous donors like yourself. *And now there's a cure.* And you lived to see it! Think of that."

He lay there with his hands bloody as he gripped his punctured belly and he tried to scream, but it hurt too much.

I leaned back against the desk and had two smokes while I watched him sob, whimper, and finally die.

But just before his lights went out, I bid him goodbye, my way.

"No, sucker," I said, "I win."

A TIP OF THE PORKPIE

Because my approach to completing Mickey Spillane's unfinished novels is to set them in the period during which he began them, I find myself working from materials that were contemporary to my famous co-author but which require me to forge a novel that is a period piece bordering on an historical novel.

In that spirit, I wish to acknowledge *Peppermint Twist* (2012) by John Johnson, Jr. and Joel Selvin with Dick Cami, for information about the legendary Peppermint Lounge. Although the Genovese crime family's involvement in the club is well-known, the treatment of the mob's role here is fictional.

I also wish to thank and acknowledge my wife Barb Collins, with whom I write a very un-Spillane-like mystery series about antiquing, who gave me two extremely important suggestions that improved this book a great deal. Thanks also to my partner Jane Spillane, Titan editor Miranda Jewess, my lost brother Nick Landau, and my friend and agent, Dominick Abel.

ABOUT THE AUTHORS

MICKEY SPILLANE and **MAX ALLAN COLLINS** collaborated on numerous projects, including twelve anthologies, three films, and the *Mike Danger* comic book series.

SPILLANE was the bestselling American mystery writer of the twentieth century. He introduced Mike Hammer in *I, the Jury* (1947), which sold in the millions, as did the six tough mysteries that soon followed. The controversial P.I. has been the subject of a radio show, comic strip, and several television series, starring Darren McGavin in the 1950s and Stacy Keach in the '80s and '90s. Numerous gritty movies have been made from Spillane novels, notably director Robert Aldrich's seminal film *noir*, *Kiss Me Deadly* (1955), and *The Girl Hunters* (1963), in which the writer played his own famous hero.

COLLINS has earned an unprecedented twenty-two Private Eye Writers of America "Shamus" nominations, winning for the novels *True Detective* (1983) and *Stolen Away* (1993) in his Nathan Heller series, and for "So Long, Chief," a Mike Hammer short story begun by Spillane and completed by Collins. His graphic novel *Road to Perdition* is the basis of the Academy Award-winning Tom Hanks/Sam Mendes film. A filmmaker in the Midwest, he has had half a dozen feature screenplays produced, including *The Last Lullaby* (2008), based on his innovative Quarry novels, also the basis of *Quarry*, a current Cinemax TV series. As "Barbara Allan," he and his wife Barbara write the "Trash 'n' Treasures" mystery series (recently *Antiques Swap*).

Both Spillane (who died in 2006) and Collins received the Private Eye Writers life achievement award, the Eye.

MIKE HAMMER NOVELS

In response to reader request, I have assembled this chronology to indicate where the Hammer novels I've completed from Mickey Spillane's unfinished manuscripts fit into the canon. An asterisk indicates the collaborative works (thus far).

M.A.C.

I, the Jury

*Lady, Go Die!**

The Twisted Thing (published 1966, written 1949)

My Gun Is Quick

Vengeance Is Mine!

One Lonely Night

The Big Kill

Kiss Me, Deadly

*Kill Me, Darling**

The Girl Hunters

The Snake

*Complex 90**

*Murder Never Knocks**

*The Big Bang**

The Body Lovers

Survival… Zero!

*Kiss Her Goodbye**

The Killing Man

Black Alley

*King of the Weeds**

*The Goliath Bone**

LADY, GO DIE!

MICKEY SPILLANE & MAX ALLAN COLLINS

Hammer and Velda go on vacation to a small beach town on Long Island after wrapping up the Williams case (*I, the Jury*). Walking romantically along the boardwalk, they witness a brutal beating at the hands of some vicious local cops—Hammer wades in to defend the victim.

When a woman turns up naked—and dead—astride the statue of a horse in the small-town city park, how she wound up this unlikely Lady Godiva is just one of the mysteries Hammer feels compelled to solve...

"Collins knows the pistol-packing PI inside and out, and Hammer's vigilante rage (and gruff way with the ladies) reads authentically." *Booklist*

"A fun read that rings true to the way the character was originally written by Spillane." *Crimespree Magazine*